Family Paradise
Sophie MacDonald
Copyright Sophie MacDonald 2013
Published at Smashwords

Family Paradise

CHAPTER 1

It was probably going to be the last family vacation we ever had, just amongst the seven of us anyway. Yeah, we had a rather large family as it eventually turned out. Early on, my father had come to meet my mother with two kids of his own by a previous marriage. His wife had died a couple of years earlier, so he brought into the relationship my two half siblings, Chrissy was six at the time, and David was four. Mom had gone through a divorce around the same time, and brought with her another stepsibling, Jessica, also four years old, same age as David. A year after they were married, I came along, named after my father Brad, though early on everyone called me "junior". That wasn't so bad, except that later "junior" became "B.J." which at the time as a young kid, I didn't associate anything with. That came later, much to my chagrin. Last but not least was Stacy, my sister, three years younger than myself, and totally unexpected as she was the only one who hadn't really been planned for. Needless to say, with such a diversity of characters and personalities we all had our moments trying to get along. Frankly I'm surprised that as kids, we didn't kill one another.

As we all grew and matured however, it seemed that as young adults, we'd finally managed to outgrow our petty differences. If anything, many of us actually growing closer to our step, or half brothers and sisters, which had certainly been the case for

Chrissy and I. Now a striking twenty seven year old woman who was starting to make a name for herself as a realtor. She had in fact taken a position with the company that she was working for out of state. As such, it was either now or never that we took this vacation, as a family while everyone was still close enough to home in order to do so. Even Stacy, the youngest had plans for attending college a goodly distance away, though still living in the same State, though it would be a long six hour drive in order to actually see her.

As diverse as we all were in our characters and personalities, the same held true for looks as well. Quite naturally, Chrissy and David looked a bit more alike with fairly dark brown, almost black hair, though somewhat fair complexions. Jessica, like mom was a very typical blue-eyed blonde, and also like mom, fairly large in the chest bust-wise, something that Chrissy wasn't. Much smaller, almost petite, at best sporting a full sized "A" cup, I know...because I had had an opportunity here and there to have seen her. Even then, I always had enjoyed seeing her tits, and as a young boy, had even fantasized about them whenever I masturbated. More on that one later.

As for myself, I was a bit more like dad. Same dark brown hair that he had, and lots of it. We shared pretty much the same build and height as well, with me just an inch below six feet and around a hundred and eighty, solidly built pounds as I'd always been active in various sports and activities all through high school. And now again while attending college myself, though at a closer, local university than the one my sister Stacy had intentions of attending.

Stacy, my true sister was more like mom. Dishwater blonde hair, just under five and a half feet, and though her bust wasn't quite as large as moms or Jessica's was, she was still amply endowed in that department too. Yeah, once again...I know, because I'd had a few opportunities to take advantage of that one as well.

Early on, while dad was still an up and coming stockbroker, we had been forced to live in a small three bedroom home. Mom and dad having one room of course, the girls the largest one...and then David and I sharing a much, much smaller bedroom with bunk beds. As kids, we never did get along. And had it not been for my size, even being four years younger than he was, I'd have been taken advantage of every step of the way. As it was, my size and build eventually put the two of us on more equal footing, though all that did was ensure one or the other of us came away with an occasional black-eye as we seemed to be constantly fighting with one another back in the day. At one point, it had gotten so bad that they'd eventually (and just temporarily) moved me into the sitting, or living room on the couch just to keep the two of us apart. As it turned out, I loved sleeping there as I'd caught more than one late night excursion from my sister, Chrissy. Turns out, she was a sleepwalker, and very often did so. And usually, naked to boot.

By the time dad finally made it big as an investment counselor for several large firms, we finally moved into a rather nice, and very large home, with each of us actually having our very own bedrooms. Though even then, we still managed to stumble into one another while getting dressed or ready for school. Stacy, Jessica and I being assigned one bathroom on the floor we slept, and Chrissy and David sharing a bathroom on the floor just below us.

The bottom line was, we got used to seeing one another in various stages of undress, sometimes purposely, sometimes teasingly, just annoying one another as siblings very often do. There really wasn't anything untoward going on amongst us, not really...not at the time anyway, though again, we all had to some extent taken a more personal confidence in our various brothers and sisters one way or another. As I had done with Chrissy, now Chris...as things turned out. For whatever reason, she had taken me under her wing perhaps as a kid, especially during the rough times I had with David, and then later...when girlfriend problems eventually came my way. That's when things got really interesting between us. Chris was the first one to actually tell me all about sex, and everything that encompassed. She had even gone so far as to let me have a "look" at it, just so I'd know what a woman's pussy actually looked like long before I ever really did anything. That was the sort of relationship we had together, though David and Jessica had much of the same thing between the two of them, as we would all eventually learn later on. Only Stacy seemed to be left out of that personal bonding, still the kid, still the youngest, and thus took haven more with our mother than anyone else. When Chris began spending more and more time outside the home, eventually moving into her own place in fact, was when Stacy and I seemed to quite naturally gravitate closer to one another. I was after all her "real" brother as she so aptly put it, and she being...my little sister, and someone I began looking out for, and protective of. She and I had the same interesting conversation about sex that Chrissy and I had had. But that was also when I discovered a shared secret she confided in me about. My younger, sweet, sexy little sister...had a thing for girls. Not that I minded, that was her business and personal preference, but you'd never have known it or suspected it to look at her. She was about as girly-girly as you could ever get, and even managed to keep her secret away from the others. Hell, she even went so far as to date boys once in a while, so it wasn't as though she was a hide-in the closet lesbian necessarily. She just simply preferred women.

But again, as I said in the beginning, the bottom line was...we were all about to venture out into our own lives, and the last opportunity we had to take advantage of one last family vacation was now. After that, we all knew we'd be calling those times something else..."family reunions" as we began bringing others into this close-knit little family. As such, mom and dad wanted to do something special, something extravagant even, especially as dad had had one of those banner years. Mom and dad spent a great deal of time thinking about it, planning it...and then came up with what they thought would be the ideal vacation get-away. At first, I wasn't too sure about it myself, but eventually the idea grew on me, along with everyone else. Mom and dad had managed to secure our own island getaway! We would figuratively, and literally be staying on our own private little island for two weeks! Though we could of course take our private launch over to the main resort island for more extravagant dinner affairs as well as shopping. The thought of spending two weeks in a tropical island paradise suddenly seemed like a dream come true, even if it would be just the seven of us sharing a small tiny island together for the majority of the time there. Mom and dad would have the main bungalow, which was much larger and had more "family" type accommodations whenever we felt like being together as a group. Thankfully, David and I would have our very own, much smaller units, though the girls were well pleased with sharing one medium sized unit amongst the three of them. All in all, everyone was well pleased and excited at the prospects, especially when the day finally came and we found ourselves winging out across the blue Pacific in search of paradise.

No one had any idea at the time, what Paradise would eventually come to represent. We would soon find out.

**

We had flown into the larger island by a small plane. Something that David and I both found exhilarating, though the girls...mom included, where quite nervous about. After we had landed and checked in, we were then escorted over to our very own private little island, which was actually less than a mile away from the larger island, yet far enough to give us a sense of welcome seclusion. Needless to say, the brochures hadn't given this place justice. It was simply unbelievable!

Each hut or bungalow basically had its own small private beach. Tall thick palm trees tended to naturally separate the view of each unit from one another, in a more or less circular pattern, though there was one area almost right in the middle of all of them that served as an open-pit fire area, and gathering area for outdoor cooking should we desire it. Beyond that, there really was plenty of privacy, and even a few hiking trails that led further into our own dense little paradise, complete with a small water fall at the far end of our two mile long little strip of ecstasy.

The first surprise came after we'd all checked in and dawned our swim-ware, mom and dad asking us to come over to their unit once we'd settled in, so that they could lay out some simple ground rules with us regarding the resort, and our stay here. Needless to say, my siblings and I were in for quite the surprise when we did. Gathering together after first checking out one another's digs...we soon headed over as a group back over to mom and dad's spacious little hut, though it certainly wasn't all that little. Extravagant to the extreme with a fully stocked bar, pantry...should we decide to cook there on the island, along with various other sundry amenities.

The thing was...they were both sitting there naked when we came in.

"Mom? Dad? You're...ah, you're...why are you naked?" Chris finally asked speaking for all of us.

"Yes...we most certainly are," mom said blushing a little. "But you might as well know, while we're here, we plan on being this way most of the time. So we wanted to come right out with it, and let you know we would be, so there wouldn't be any unexpected surprises. This trip is very special for us too, and we have every intention of taking advantage of it, even with the five of you here." Mom told us, though dad soon added to that.

"You're all adults now yourselves," he'd begun. "And it's not like we haven't run into one another in various states of undress either. So let's also act and be adults about that as well. We're here to have fun, relax, and just simply be ourselves. Your mother and I have every intention of doing just that. And our being naked is part of it. So...get used to it. Either that, or stay in your own areas if seeing the "old folks" naked tends to bother you," he actually then chuckled easing the sudden tension dramatically.

I noticed Chris was smiling as she stood there, though the rest of us were acting a bit more nervously and unsure of this sudden turn of events. Like dad said, it wasn't as though we hadn't occasionally run into one another in the all together from time to time. Nudity never really had been an issue amongst any of us while growing up. But seeing mom and dad so prominently displayed in their birthday suits went a little beyond that.

"What about us?" Chris asked, once again speaking for all of us, though to be honest about it, up until the moment she asked, even seeing mom and dad in the buff, the thought of doing the same myself really hadn't entered my mind until she brought the subject up.

"That's up to you," mom answered. "Like your dad said, we're all adults here. If you're comfortable running around our little island naked, then do it. We're certainly not hypocrites, if that's something you personally decide to do. Just keep in mind that whatever you do do...or don't, is no one else's business. And the only other thing we do ask is this...if you see the door to our bungalow closed...go away, don't bother us. It means we're having some special alone time," mom finished, though Jessica snickered, whispering just under her breath to Chris who was standing next to her.

"Fucking, they mean," she laughed, though I'd over heard her as well standing on the other side, with images of my own parents now doing the nasty together invading my thoughts. It was time to leave mom and dad to their own amusements, naked or not...and do a little bit of exploring here myself.

Mom and dad soon ushered us out, closing their door behind us as the five of us slowly meandered our way back to our own huts, though surprisingly, Chris walked beside me as I headed back to my own little place.

"You want to come exploring with me?" I asked.

"Yeah, I'd like that...provided you don't mind seeing me naked too," she informed me. I nearly tripped over my own feet when she said that.

"You serious? You're going "native" too?" I asked.

"Unless it bothers you," she informed me, already reaching behind, undoing the clasp on the bikini top she was wearing, undoing it...though holding it against herself even as it came undone, still covering her somewhat small, but very perky breasts.

"It probably will bother me...in a good way," I said teasing her back. "So long as you don't mind your brother walking around with a boner most of the day," I said not really meaning it, though half worried I actually might should she decide to get completely naked, and spend most of the time that way, not to mention the rest of my siblings.

"Not like I haven't seen it before," she reminded me. Which she had, just as she had shown me her pussy once out of curiosity, I had in kind returned the favor, though I hadn't been erect at the time either. Not that time anyway. "Interesting too," she then added before I could respond to that. "You notice how similar you and dad are in that department?"

"Not really no...I wasn't actually checking him out, though admittedly, I sort of was giving mom a good looking over. She really is quite an attractive looking woman at her age isn't she?"

"Yeah, she is...wish I had as big of tits as she and the other girls do," Chris said, just then lowering her arms, allowing her small breasts to spring free as she now carried the bikini top in her hand as we just then reached my own small little bungalow. It had actually been a while since I'd last seen them, and honestly, I think they had actually grown just a little. Chris's boobs, though small, were nicely shaped, with a slight upward pointy lift to them both. Each capped by a delicious looking, almost strawberry colored nipple, that even now seemed all hard and crinkly as she stood there.

"I like the way your tits look," I said looking at them, and then at her, seeing her blush a little, though smiling.

"Well glad you do anyway...you always were trying to get a look at them every chance you got while growing up, always thought it was cute, and yes...even a bit flattering that you wanted to with everyone else having far larger breasts than I did."

"Hell sis...you're forgetting. You also let me have a good long look at your pussy too, don't forget that. And I also think, especially now that I'm a bit more experienced in that department, that you've got the cutest, prettiest pussy I've ever seen."

"Really? You really mean that? Or are you just saying that trying to comfort me?" She asked.

"No...I mean it, you really do, though admittedly, it has been a while now since I saw it last," I added almost hopefully. Though she had indeed removed her top, I honestly didn't think she was actually considering wandering about the island in the altogether the way mom and dad planned on doing. Which is when I got the second surprise of the day, when she suddenly reached down, untying the small bows on either side of her bikini bottoms, letting them fall. Suddenly, Chris too was standing before me entirely naked. The one thing that was different now, than what I had seen before, was she was entirely bald. The last time I had seen her, once more sleep-walking, though that had been a couple of years ago now, was she'd had a bit of a pubic patch sitting there between her legs. Now...there was nothing.

I think I swallowed, standing there looking at it...at her.

"Well? You like it like this? Or not?" She suddenly asked. I swallowed again, looking up at her and then answered.

"It's...gorgeous!" I said simply, meaning it. And I knew by the way I'd said it, she knew I had meant it too. She grinned.

"Ok, so...shall we go exploring then?" She asked changing the subject. I looked down at myself, still trying to decide what to do here. Problem was, I was actually starting to grow just a little. Seeing where I was looking, she laughed. "Don't worry about it...been a while since I've see 'It' that way too," she giggled again. "But I am sure, once we start walking and just exploring, you'll find it won't be poking out quite that way as we do that. So come on BJ..." She said tossing out the name that only she had ever really gotten away with in calling me by. "Take em off...and let's go see our island!"

**

Unfortunately, I did start off sporting a partial woody, it couldn't be helped, though Chris made it easier on me by not looking at me too often, or commenting on it. By the time we had actually started the gradual slow easy climb up to where the water fall was reported to be, it had actually become considerably more flaccid, though remaining somewhat thicker than usual even then.

"There...listen, you can hear it," she informed me excitedly, now taking my hand, almost pulling me along behind her as we made our way up to the summit of the small hill. The crash of the falls just off to one side as we crept along the plateau heading towards it, winding our way in and out of the palm trees as we did that. Reaching the edge of the cliff looking down over the side, we could see it. That and the beautiful blue almost crystal clear pool some twenty or thirty feet just below us. It was the most beautiful amazing sight I had ever seen, and then Chris and I both saw another one. Not too surprisingly, Jessica and Stacy had decided to go exploring themselves. But what was surprising, was the fact that they too had obviously decided to adopt mom and dad's reasoning. They too were naked, frolicking about us just below in the water, though for the moment at least, totally oblivious to our presence having come in from the other way. I almost called out to them, but then Chris hushed me, suddenly slinking down out of sight, pulling me down with her.

"No...wait, give it a moment," she spoke, once more peering over the side, still looking around, no doubt wondering where David was, just as I now was, in thinking about it.

"He must have remained behind," I offered not seeing him, though once more looking down at the other two as they playfully swam about, splashing one another. Once more I almost called out, until I saw something...looked again, wondering if I had in fact seen what I thought I had. Once more looking over towards my sister. But her look confirmed she'd seen it too, or had at least been aware of it. Now standing together, facing one another in just a few feet of water I sat watching Stacy as she reached up, cupping one of Jessica's big firm breasts, playing with it, and then likewise fingering our sister's nipple.

"Holy shit!" I exclaimed, glad that the thunder of the falls easily concealed my sudden surprised outburst.

"Surely you've known!" Chris stated looking towards me, though her eyes spoke the question more so than her words.

"About Stacy being a lesbian? Or bi at least? Yes...but certainly not that," I said looking back down and over the cliff face towards them again, as Jessica too now held one of Stacy's breasts in her hand, likewise fondling and playing with it. "How long has this been going on?" I asked my sister.

"About a year now I think...though up until now at least, it's been more playful curiosity than anything really serious. Looks to me like, they're just taking advantage of the moment to indulge themselves just a little. I too have always known that Stacy tended to lean more towards girls than boys, but Jessica was a bit of a surprise, knowing how boy crazy she's always been. I think for her, it's more of that naughty curiosity....you know how she is, has always been. Always the first one to do or try anything, which damn near landed her in quite a bit of trouble a few times."

That was true about her for damn sure. She'd gotten busted, grounded for a couple of months for smoking pot inside the house, and was also the only one as far as I knew, who mom and dad had actually caught having sex with her boyfriend in her bed when no one was expected home. She'd been grounded for that one too.

Seeing them standing there fondling one another's breasts was hot enough, but then as they both reached down just below the surface of the water, hands between one another's legs, it became clearly obvious as to what else they were now doing.

"Are they..."

"Fingering one another? Yes...I think so," Chris half moaned watching them just as I was, though I now glanced over and realized, Chris had her own hand down between her legs, and was almost nonchalantly fingering herself, right there in front of me. In no time at all...I felt my prick suddenly stiffening to full staff, and just as she was now doing, I began doing to myself, sitting there beside my sister, the two of us touching ourselves, looking down, watching our sister's as they in turn stood fingering one another.

Sure, I had in fact masturbated a few times fantasizing about my own sisters, though most usually Chris as it turned out. And though we had on occasion played "touchy-feely" years past, we'd never really done anything, certainly nothing like this, not actually playing with myself in front of her at least, which I was most certainly doing now, and which she too was doing.

When she reached over and suddenly grasped my cock, it seemed almost natural and normal for her to do that, especially under the circumstances. Still fingering herself with one hand, and me with the other, I was content for the moment at least to just let her do that. Besides...I now had breasts to play with, and with that particular door now seemingly open, I just reached over, cupping one of them. I quickly found one of those incredibly hard, amazing nipples of hers and began fingering it, pinching it gently between my fingers as my sister began doing the same to my dick head. Sensations of her doing that, sending tingling thrills and shivers up and down my spine, causing me to shake with excitement uncontrollably.

"You keep doing that...you're gonna make me..."

"Cum?" Chris quipped. "God, I certainly hope so...admittedly Brad, I've always wanted to see you do that. I don't mind telling you, I used to lay there in bed at night and fantasize about you...fantasize about what it might be like...being with you. Does that shock you?" She said now looking at me worriedly, not to mention that her hand had also stopped stroking my dick.

"God Chris! Don't stop now! I'm so fucking close!" I told her. "And just so you know...I spent many a night in my own bed, thinking about you too!"

We both turned as one, once more looking down over the cliff, the echoing sounds of our sister's mutual release as the water amplified their cries of joy. The two hugging one another closely now, still furiously, even more so perhaps....finger-fucking one another as first Jessica cried out, and then Stacy did. Gradually slowing, stepping back slightly from one another, YET kissing one another softly for a moment. They turned, though still holding hands as they walked back up towards the small beach where their towels were. I more or less missed that last part however, my eyes were closed, as though glued shut. At the moment I was too busy pouring what felt like a gallon of semen down my sister's throat. It was the third, and best surprise of the day as I had started to cum, and then suddenly her mouth was surrounding me, drinking me down, swallowing my essence as it began exploding from the tip of my cock. Nothing else mattered at the moment...not even my other horny naughty naked sisters.

By the time I was able to open my eyes and stand up straight again, Jessica and Stacy had disappeared, no doubt heading back towards their bungalow again. We'd all been gone for the better part of two hours now, and it was likewise time for the two of us to head back in order to get dressed for dinner as we'd actually be heading over to the main island in order to do that.

"Are we ok?" Chris asked somewhat nervously, still licking her lips, a reminder that she'd just finished draining my balls. My own sister...had sucked me wonderfully dry.

"More than," I assured her, actually kissing her, which surprised her a little. She hadn't expected that, nor had I actually, only then realizing I was tasting my own cum inside her mouth, at least the residue of it as I did, as our tongues briefly fenced one another for a moment. "Let's just say...I owe you one," I said grinning at her, though my hand had almost automatically come up to gently grasp and fondle one of her small perky breasts again, causing her to moan pleasurably as I did that.

"I'm going to hold you to that," she told me. "Later, after we get back from dinner," she stated. The two of us suddenly now glad that David and I had our own private little bungalows, making it a hell of a lot easier for the two of us to do something like that.

"I'll make it worth your while too," I assured her, feeling myself growing hard and stiff again even though I'd just had one of the most amazing, most intense orgasms of my entire life. And this time, I walked all the way back to the bungalows like that too. My prick never did go down...though walking behind Chris as she more or less pulled me a long behind her sort of kept it that way.

**

Chris and I finally parted heading off in our own separate directions just as we reached the edge of the semi-circular formation of huts. I walked inside, wondering what Chris would say...if anything to our sisters, especially upon realizing that she'd left her bikini behind at my place. I was still grinning from ear to ear, surprised and delighted by the unexpected turn of events as I stepped beneath the shower, which was also outside. The water naturally warmed and heated by the sun as I stood there beneath it, showering. Images of what we had seen and done so recently together filling my mind, so much so that it took a moment to realize I was hearing David's voice as he stood there speaking to me.

"Hey!" He finally said a bit louder, sort of hanging over the side of my shower enclosure looking down at me. For once I was actually grateful I wasn't sporting a hard on.

"What?" I responded back, adding...'Where've you been anyway?" I asked curiously. He just grinned at me, looking like the cat that had eaten the canary. Though the two of us had never really gotten close, especially with all the earlier animosity between us, at least as we'd grown and matured, we'd set most of those petty differences aside. At least now we were far more civil to one another...well sort of anyway. I could tell he was dying to tell me what he'd been up to. That look I HAD seen before.

"Guess what I saw?" He asked trying to bait me, which was his way. I was half tempted to say the same thing back to him, deciding against it however. I figured mine was a hell of a lot better than his was, and for the moment at least, was keeping that one to myself.

"What?" I said instead, stepping out of the shower, grabbing a towel as I began drying off.

"Earlier? I went back to lie down, take a nap for a bit. When I woke up a short time later, everyone had already taken off of course."

"Yeah? So?"

"Well, I was naturally hungry, so I headed back towards mom and dad's hut, the door was open now, so I figured they weren't inside doing anything, and that it was safe to go in, browse around, find something to munch on."

That was typically David. He seemed to have a bottomless pit when it came to snacking, though he also had the metabolism for it too. He never did gain any weight, no matter what it was he seemed to be eating, unlike myself.

"Yeah? So?" I said again, this time showing some irritation in saying it, wanting him to get on with it instead of drawing things out the way he usually did. He got the point.

"They said not to come in or bother them when the door was closed right? Well, they didn't warn us, or tell us they might do something elsewhere now did they?"

He had my attention now, curiously enough.

While I was making a sandwich, I looked outside, spotted them laying on their own little beach there. Next thing I know, mom reaches over, starts playing with dad's dick, and then suddenly she's giving him a BJ, B.J.," he says grinning at me. I let it go this time however, without commenting on that.

"So...you watched mom giving dad a blowjob huh?"

"Watched em fucking too," he then added as though this was the real reason for the canary look. I didn't have the heart to tell him. Nor did I really want to. "Bet you've never seen them doing that now have you?"

"Nope...you're one up on me there David," I smiled back. "But I will say this, we've what...been here less than a day already? I have a feeling we'll both be seeing that, and perhaps a bit more...so don't be surprised by it if you do. And more importantly, don't make an issue out of it either, if you do...otherwise, you might bring an end to it. And I don't think either one of us would want anything like that to happen, now would we?"

He thought about that for a moment, shaking his head in agreement with it. "Still pretty cool though, sick and twisted as it might be...watching mom and dad actually fucking. Don't mind telling you Brad, it really was pretty hot."

"I hear you," I told him, now picturing it in my own mind, remembering what mom actually looked like, and now finding myself actually getting a bit aroused here. "But...like I said, just don't be too surprised by things around here David. We've got two full weeks here, who knows what the hell might happen while we are?"

He looked at me speculatively, smiled knowingly nodding his head. "God...one can only imagine, and hope," he added grinning like a Cheshire cat.

I had to agree with him on that one.

**

We took the launch over to the main island shortly before the sun went down. It was an enjoyable dinner, sitting there on the veranda, a nice tropical breeze blowing, as we sat sipping Mai tais together. Just watching the sunset over the Pacific Ocean was breathtaking enough in and of itself. But sitting there looking at four, yes four, very attractive, and obviously very sensual women, simply added to the majestic scenery of the evening.

After we finished watching the sun sink far off into the sea, we took a stroll around the resort, stopping to window shop. There was a club with dancing, which mom and dad of course wanted to do, as did most everyone else including me. All save for Stacy who had been acting a little strangely most of the night. Not so much that anyone else had really noticed, but I had. Especially when I saw her resigned look at the mention that mom and dad planned on staying at the club for a while. I could tell she wasn't too keen on the idea.

"Tired?" I asked.

"Yes!" She said hopefully, as though wishing that someone might in fact take her back to our own little island. I made mention of the fact to everyone that she was, and then offered to take her back, and then actually come back for everyone else at a specific time, not wanting to leave her all alone on the island either. I too feigned being tired, even though I wasn't, so it was agreed that I'd return at midnight. Just before I left however, dad came back informing me that they would be taking the resort launch back, so I didn't have to worry about doing that. As such, Stacy and I soon headed back without much being said along the way. I could tell however that something was bothering her.

Walking back to her bungalow, I wasn't at all surprised when she invited me inside.

"What's troubling you sis? And don't tell me nothing is, I know...something is, I could see it in your eyes all evening."

"You always could," she responded knowingly. "I never was one to be able to hide anything from you was I?"

"Nope! So, tell me...what gives sis?"

Stacy plopped down on one of the really comfortable looking beds, and then patted at a spot next to her, which I took, sitting down beside her.

"I want to ask you something."

"Shoot."

"Was it you...or David, that was sitting on top of the plateau earlier today?" She asked straight out.

Obviously she had seen me after all, though curiously, she'd made no mention of anyone else, so I didn't either. "It was me," I answered directly leaving it at that. She actually smiled, even giving a small sigh of relief upon hearing that.

"Good...that's a relief," she smiled almost brazenly, yet blushing simultaneously at the same time. "I wasn't sure. When Jessica and I walked back up to the beach, I happened to glance up, saw someone...but the sunlight was partially blocking my view. I knew someone had seen us, obviously a male...but wasn't sure beyond that. Obviously..." she paused for a moment, even reaching over to place her hand on my bare thigh. "You saw us."

"I did, yes." I said easily enough, enjoying the sensation of her hand on my thigh, the sudden unexpected intimacy of such a simple act.

"Were you...you know," she stammered slightly, her hand now softly circling, caressing my thigh gradually inching upwards as she did that.

"Jerking off?" I answered back, speaking truthfully to some extent as I pictured the moment in my head. I had been...up until the moment that Chris suddenly leaned over taking my cock into her mouth anyway. Which is no doubt why Stacy hadn't seen anyone else sitting up there with me.

"Yeah, that," she giggled then, her hand actually brushing over the now growing bulge of my cock through my loose fitting shorts.

Stacy and I too had played those "I'll show you mine, if you'll show me yours," games when we were younger. And she also had the distinction of being the only one amongst all of my siblings (not counting my mother) who had actually caught me in the act of masturbating. The day she had, I'd been in the bathroom just coming out from a shower. Since we shared a shower, and as there was rarely any time to do anything in there, especially clean up before someone else was pounding on the door wanting to use it, I never jerked off in there. I stood, one hand on the wall behind the toilet leaning forward, legs slightly spread, hand on my cock jerking away, pointing it downwards towards the toilet bowl. I hadn't locked the door, nor did anyone really. Had I done so, the girls too would have no doubt gotten into the habit of locking it as well in retaliation for my doing that. Keeping it unlocked had become somewhat of a game we all played on one another from time to time. The unexpected sudden quick walk in, glimpses here, there, while in the shower or just getting out. It was relatively harmless, and everyone did it from time to time. But that day...I knew I had been alone, the last one to leave, or so I thought anyway.

So I wasn't too worried about anyone coming in unexpectedly. In addition to that, I was so lost in my thoughts, my fantasies, the "edge" of release already beginning to seize my balls when Stacy knocked, (which we always did as quick fare warning) however, I hadn't heard the faint knock, nor the door opening at that moment as my cock began to spurt, almost the exact moment she came in. Stacy stood (though I didn't even know that at the time) watching me, watching me squirt off into the toilet, yanking my prick pleasurably, groaning and moaning deeply as I did so. Images of her in fact, even then filling my head. As I finally opened my eyes, still peering down into the bowl of the toilet to take stock of what felt like one hell of a load, Stacy finally spoke, startling me.

"Wow...so that's what it looks like when it comes out huh?"

I think I jumped three feet. "Jesus...fuck...Stacy!" I spat suddenly turning trying to cover myself, though the damage was done. Even more so when Stacy walked over, looking down into the very toilet bowl herself likewise inspecting the discharge of cream that now floated there like clouds in the sky.

I reached over, flushing it. Though we both now stood there watching the swirl of water as my cum-curdles fought vainly to remain behind.

"Sorry...it's just that, I've never seen that before," she finally stated. "I mean...I know boys cum and all, but I've never actually seen one do it before. It was...well, it was rather interesting," she stated now looking up towards me.

"Well, I guess you have now," I stated finding the moment suddenly arousing in a weird sort of way, though I began wrapping a towel around my still somewhat stiff member by way of hiding it.

She just stood there looking at me though, the question in her eyes without speaking.

"What?"

She remained silent for a moment more, the anguish of her thoughts clearly etched within her face. "Can I...can I see you do it again?"

"What...you mean, jerk off again, while you watch?" I asked frankly surprised by this, though not without a bit of mild amusement, not to mention aroused interest as my cock actually throbbed just a bit upon hearing that.

"Yes." She said simply, obviously serious about it.

"Shit...I don't know sis. Maybe. But certainly not now. It you know...takes a while. And if you really, honestly do want to see that, you're going to have to give it time. If I was to do it now...there wouldn't be a whole lot to see since I pretty much emptied my balls here."

She laughed at that. "When then? Tonight?"

I thought about it. Aside from Jessica being home, mom and dad had their weekly card game with the neighbors. David would be at work, and Chris was living in her own place at the time.

"Yeah, later tonight maybe," I had told her as the thought of jerking off for my sister again suddenly started to arouse me. I had done so of course...seeing the excitement in her eyes as she sat across from me, watching me jerk off until my prick once more erupted copiously for her.

Returning back to the present however, Stacy's hand still making soft gentle circles on my thigh, I looked at her wondering. "So...what did you think?" She suddenly asked. "Did you enjoy seeing us? Did you like what you saw? Did you cum?" She finished, her breath sounding excited, obviously aroused.

"It was hot sis. Admittedly. So yeah, I enjoyed watching you. And yeah...I did cum hard. Very...very hard." I added.

I now felt her hand actually grasp me even though it was through the material of my shorts. The fact she'd even done this surprised me just a little, I started to say something, to respond in some way to her action, but she quickly headed me off.

"Please Brad, please. I've been thinking about doing this ever since this morning," she began. "I want to watch you, see you...cum again. But this time, I want to be the one that makes it do it," she said beginning to unzip my fly. If I'd had any resolve, any misgivings about any of this, about her...especially being my true sister, they went right out the door. The moment I felt the softness of her hand touch the hardness of my aching stiff cock, I was gone.

"Here, let's make this easier for both of us," I told her, now standing undoing my shorts, slipping them off completely. I hadn't worn underwear, so I was immediately naked from the waist down, but I didn't stop there either, quickly pulling my tee shirt up and over my head. "Your turn," I now said looking at her as I stood there in front of her completely naked now.

"Me?"

"Yes...you. I want to look at you while you do this," I said simply. This time she didn't even hesitate, quickly pulling off her blouse, and just as quickly her bra, then her own shorts until she was finally wearing nothing more than a pair of light blue bikini panties. These too she then slid down her own legs, until we were both standing there only a few feet apart, looking at one another totally and completely naked since the first time we'd done this as children simply curious about one another. I knew however, there was going to be a lot more happening than simply looking at one another this time.

Stacy had an incredible body. More so than I actually realized. I found I was even jealous of it just a little, her stomach taut, flat...her abs clearly defined, honed and toned. She wore what was typically I suppose called a small tiny landing strip above her pubic area. Just a small, neatly trimmed tuft of heavenly fur. Her belly button was pierced, a small diamond stud actually catching the moonlight as it drifted in through the window, causing it to glimmer suggestively. Above, as my eyes travelled onward in rapturous exploration of my younger, sexy sister, her full breasts, easily a nice B cup stood full, well-rounded and heavy against her chest. Her nipples appeared to be a light brown, perhaps even tan in color. Areolas as large as a fifty-cent piece, though her nipples were thick, standing atop each one in obvious arousal. I found myself reaching out, my hands suddenly capturing each one of them between my fingers without even asking her permission in doing so. She gave it, with a deep growly moan as I stood there caressing her breasts, teasing her nipple tips, and felt as my hard stiff cock now throbbed anxiously against her tummy. Feeling it as well perhaps, she reached down, once more grasping it within her hand as she stood there gingerly toying with it, exploring it, as I stood exploring her.

"Sit down," she said pushing me back onto the bed, forced to release her, though she quickly joined me again, crawling up by my side.

"Turn around," I said in kind. "If you're going to play with me...I'm going to play with you."

Stacy giggled excitedly, quickly switching positions so that we were laying head to toe on our sides. Almost immediately she was back to fondling and toying with my cock as I likewise began strumming her preciously wet slit.

"So tell me sis...how long have you and Jessica been fooling around?" I asked running my finger up her tender groove, just brushing her glistening hard little clit. She shivered, moaned involuntarily, telling me in a heartbeat just how aroused she really was.

"About a year now I guess," she barely managed. "It's not like we do things a lot, just once in a while. Usually...when she's between boyfriends, like she is now. I can almost plan on her coming to me whenever she's gone through a breakup. Sort of like recharging her batteries."

"And what about your batteries? You like it when she recharges yours?"

"Admittedly I do Brad. But then again, I think you've always known I have a particular fondness for women. Not that I don't enjoy something like this once in a while too, just not many men out there I'm particularly attracted to. Though admittedly, being attracted to my own brother isn't probably the smartest thing in the world to be doing, not to mention likewise being attracted to my own sisters too."

"Sisters? As in both Jessica and Chris?"

Stacy blushed profusely. "Ooops! God Brad! Please don't say anything to her about that. It's supposed to be a secret. Not even Jessica knows that Chris and I used to fool around some when she was living at home too. She's the one that actually taught me how to masturbate, and was the first pussy I ever actually went down on. It's been a long time since we've actually done anything though...and admittedly I do miss it." She paused, holding but not stroking my cock as she leaned up looking at me. "So...what do you think about all this Brad? Am I horrible? Do you think I'm a bad person because I find more enjoyment and excitement playing with my own brothers and sisters than I do anyone else?"

"Bad in a good way," I responded back. "You make me wanna be bad too sis. Really bad. Bad to the point that I'd like to do more than just finger your pussy if you know what I mean."

"I'm ah....I'm still a virgin Brad," she suddenly confessed. "Believe it or not, that's something I still haven't experienced. Though maybe I'm technically not a virgin any more, not like I still have my hymen, it's just that..."

"You've never had a man's cock inside you," I finished for her.

"Exactly."

"Are you...considering it then?"

"I don't know...maybe. With the right person maybe."

"Have anyone in mind?"

She grabbed my cock firmly once more, stroking it vigorously again. "Sort of...I'm still considering it," she smiled at me, and then surprised the hell out of me as she stuck out her tongue licking the head of my prick for a moment. I figured that all was fair game, as I likewise leaned forward a bit more myself, quickly running my own tongue up and down that wet slippery split of hers. I began teasing that hard little nubbin as she suddenly groaned, one hand coming down to rest on the back of my head as I continued licking and lapping away at her.

"Oh fuck...yes Brad, yes. Eat my pussy baby...eat your naughty sister's horny hot cunt!"

As horny as she was, it didn't take long. Within moments, Stacy was bouncing, quivering and almost spasmodically thrashing about beside me as her legs suddenly locked around my head. Drawing her clit even deeper into my mouth, I rolled it around with my lips and tongue until she screamed out, exploding in a series of orgasmic tidal waves that all but put her into a catatonic state afterwards. Finally too tender to touch any more, she pushed me away, curling up into a fetal position, still quivering and shaking as I curled up behind her, simply holding her until she simply fell asleep. I laughed silently. Her intention to see me cum, make me cum...which I hadn't as yet, as I quietly slid out of bed, covering her with the simple plain sheet before making my way back to my own bungalow. I had barely made it back, crawling into my own bed when the sound of the resorts launch approaching our little island reached my ears. I soon drifted off into my own restful sleep, thoughts of my dear sweet little sister filling my head as I did.

**

I couldn't have been asleep very long, even as tired as I was after a rather intense and exciting first day. But it was the hushed giggled coming from David's hunt a short distance away from my own that shook me from sleep. After all, it wasn't David who was doing the giggling.

With mom and dad's bungalow on the other side of mine, and much further away than David's was, I doubted that anyone else could have possibly heard those sounds. Even the girls hut was as far away from David's place as was mom and dads, but that begged the question. "What was going on anyway?" Finding my watch, I realized that barely an hour had passed before they had obviously returned. By now, everyone else was no doubt fast asleep, all except for David of course, and by the sounds of the female giggles I had heard, it sounded as though it was Jessica who was with him. Now curious, I rolled out of bed, still naked in fact, and silently walked down the small dirt path towards his hut. A full moon easily lit the way, though the only sound I could now hear was the gentle waves crashing on the tiny island beach surrounding us.

Though the door to David's hut was closed, the open air window wasn't. Making my way stealthily off to the side, I approached, sliding up next to the window itself which was large and easily chest height. I took a quick peek inside, glad that the moonlight was bathing the inside of the room just enough in order to see by as I did. Aside from that, they had no other lights on. But it wasn't necessary anyway, I could clearly see well enough as to what was going on.

Jessica was naked, kneeling on the bed with David behind her. I stood there looking in, watching my sister's tits swinging to and fro wildly as David fucked her from behind. Even in the subdued light, I could still easily see his rather impressive looking member sliding in and out of my sister's pussy. He slowed, teasing her...withdrawing it just as slowly, and then ramming it home fully and deeply into her, withdrawing slowly again, repeating the exquisite torture.

"You fuck!" She said looking back, reaching down between her legs as though to capture him and make him speed up again. "Quit teasing me! I'm almost there...again," she laughed. "Hurry up you bitch!" She called him. "Fuck me! Fuck me hard...deep and fast you little shit!"

"This entire family's going to hell in a hand basket!" I mused. "Now just how long has THIS been going on?" I asked myself wondering if Jessica wasn't indeed the main instigator of all this, though also asking myself just as suddenly..."If she is...then why hasn't she approached me as well?"

Though curious about that, I was still rather horny myself from my earlier enjoyment's with Stacy. Now standing there outside their window, watching the two of them as David finally began complying with my sister's wishes. He was soon slamming into her wildly from behind, the sounds of flesh slapping against flesh as David now pulled out all the stops and began fucking Jessica furiously. I continued to watch, now feeling my own orgasm begin to make an appearance, once more smiling to myself as I looked down and around, spotting a nearby chair I could use to stand on. Retrieving it, I moved it next to the window, stood on it, though not before ensuring those two were too busy to see me. Satisfied they were, though not for much longer by the sounds and looks of it, I stood on the chair, pointed my cock through the open window and proceeded to jerk myself off. Several hard-tossed ribbons of sperm flew in to the darkness, landing god knows where as they did. Pleased with myself at a bit of brotherly retaliation I suppose, I climbed back down again just as I heard them both squealing rapturously in their own climatic bliss. Returning the chair back to where I had found it, I made my way back to my own hut again, this time falling into a deep restful sleep until the warmth of the early morning sunlight finally awakened me.

**

Rolling out of bed once again, I quickly took a much needed pee, and then stepped out into my own cozy little porch. Though the sun was fully up, it was early yet. But even then I knew my dad would be up as well, already having made, and no doubt drinking coffee perhaps. I quickly began walking in that direction, suddenly stopping taking stock of the fact that I didn't have a single stitch on! I almost turned to head back, and then bravely thought better of it. "Fuck...why should I care if they don't?" I asked myself. Boldly I continued on, not at all surprised to see that dad was indeed sitting out on their own comfy little porch facing the beach. He was indeed drinking coffee, and just as naked as I was as I came up and stood there next to him.

"Morning son, sleep well?" He asked, adding. "Coffee's ready if you want some."

"Like a log," I responded back, already turning to head inside to the kitchenette they had. "Where's mom?"

"You know her," he told me. "Already gone for her morning run, with Stacy and Chris as it appears. They should be coming back around any time now in fact. There's an easy little jogging path that's half a mile around the huts here. Four laps will give her, her two mile run," he said peering down the beach. "Ah...there they are now," he said pointing. I looked, just making them out as they headed our way. Time enough to walk inside, pour myself a cup and rejoin him, which I did, just as David arrived.

"Ah, thanks Bro," David said reaching for my cup, though I easily ducked him, side-stepping him.

"Get your own," I admonished him, only then realizing that he too was as naked as I was. Definitely, something about being here on this little island had seemed to evaporate whatever modesty or inhibitions any of us might have had. Taking a seat, I sat down sipping my coffee as David soon joined us, taking a seat up on the other side of dad as the three of us now sat watching the girls grow ever closer towards us as they ran.

All three of them were naked too.

"Interesting life here isn't it?" Dad mused watching the girls slowly jogging, though we were too. With them only a hundred or so yards away from us now, seeing the gentle bounce of mom and Stacy's breasts was mildly amusing, though more so perhaps the fact that Chris's boobs weren't moving at all of course, small as they were. But even then, it was arousing to be sitting there watching the three of them as they approached.

Mom was smiling, and even waved as they drew closer to us, calling out. "Only two more to go!" She grinned acknowledging the three of us as the three of them soon passed us, continuing on their little early morning jog. As one, the three of us sat, heads turned following, now watching three very shapely asses as they continued on down the beach, though Stacy took a moment to look back in our direction. I think I caught a faint smile on her face as she did that before turning back around again. Looking away from them, I just caught dad's hand down in his lap, he had in fact...for the moment at least, actually been fondling himself. And though not quite erect, he was proportionally a bit bigger than he had been a moment ago. As though realizing this, he'd taken his hand away from himself, once more reaching for his coffee, only then looking at me. Though I too had lifted my own cup back to my lips sipping from it looking oblivious about the obvious.

"Pleasant little sight that, wasn't it?" He grinned somewhat awkwardly. Though I couldn't help but agree with him, it had been. Though it was David who was even more obvious about it than we were. His cock had risen considerably, no longer flaccid, and now poking out quite a bit, far more so than even dads had been.

"Obviously, your brother enjoyed it too," Dad quipped suddenly aware of David's stiff standing erection. "Nothing to be ashamed of either son," he told him then. "Just our way of quietly appreciating the beauty of the women in this family," he stated then. Which was when Jessica suddenly came walking up.

"What's this about the beautiful women in this family?" She asked walking up to dad, kissing him on the cheek, and then stealing his coffee away from him, sipping it. Her large breasts mere inches away from dad's face as she did that, me...chuckling to myself as dad's gaze never wavered from them either, not even aware as yet that she had taken his coffee cup and was drinking from it.

"How come you're not running with the rest of them?" I asked as Jessica handed dad's cup back to him, which he accepted, only then tearing his eyes away from her exposed breasts. I noticed in the brief moment he did that, his cock had now stiffened, though he soon crossed his legs in an effort to partially conceal that at least.

"I'm not much of a jogger for one thing. But for another, I'm not about to run naked like the three of them either," she said suddenly cupping both breasts within her hands. "These things tend to get in the way without some form of support. Frankly I'm surprised mom and Stacy are out there running like that too." Dad laughed at that.

"Actually, mom was in fact holding her breasts earlier the first time she came around, so maybe they were bothering her just a bit," dad conceded.

"Maybe...she was just playing with them," David quipped, likewise eye-balling his own sister as she stood there, visions for me now...of the two of them fucking one another in David's hut last night. I was half tempted to ask him if he'd discovered any strange snail markings on his floor this morning, but then thought better of it.

"Well, one thing's for sure, I plan on doing just that a bit later on today," dad remarked almost proudly of the fact that he at least was actually getting some. Little did he know of course. "So...what are your plans for the day anyway?" He then asked the three of us.

"Well I for one, want to go back over to the resort, do some shopping and maybe even a little gambling in the casino later. Anyone feel like coming with me?" She asked. Though I too was interested in doing that, I had already promised Stacy that we'd go for a swim later in the pool below the falls. David however answered before I did.

"I do!" He told her. "I want to see if I have any better luck than I did last night," he then added.

"Just see to it you don't spend all your money foolishly," dad cautioned him. "Cause you're not getting any more from me this trip," he then added. "This trips already cost me a small fortune as it is...though it's well worth it," he then added to that as once more the girls rounded the corner down the beach from us again, heading back this way. "If you know what I mean, he added to that." We all looked, and then we all laughed. This time, it was Stacy who was jogging while holding her own boobs in her hands.

"See? That's why," Jessica chuckled again. "Told you."

This time as they drew close to us though, Stacy dropped out, mom and Chris continuing on for their last lap.

"Next time...I'm wearing a bra," she stated walking over to us, though once more giving me what could only be taken as a special knowing little look as she said that. She even brushed by me, her hand just grazing my cock briefly, though well out of sight from anyone seeing her having done that. Even so, I was surprised she had even attempted it with everyone standing around like they were.

"Come on David...let's get dressed and head over to the island," Jessica said. "Grab some breakfast, do some shopping, and then gamble a bit. You want to come with us Stacy?" She then asked.

"Ah...no, no thanks. I'm thinking about going back up to the falls here in a little bit for a swim, maybe next time." Jessica looked at me then, though without saying anything and just smiled.

"Ah huh...well, enjoy yourselves," she then added, including me in that though I hadn't said anything. Thankfully, both she and David soon headed off to actually get dressed.

"Want something to eat?" Stacy asked both dad and I.

"No thanks honey, already had some fruit and pastries myself this morning. Plenty more inside though if you're hungry. Thanks anyway."

Stacy and I quickly headed inside in order to do just that. "What would you like to eat?" She turned almost the moment we got inside out of earshot, her hand already coming down to rap itself around my somewhat stiff member. "I know what I'd like to eat," she said picking up a banana, and seductively peeling it then before wrapping her lips around most of its entire length. "Which reminds me...I sort of owe you one don't I? We never did finish what I had wanted to do in the beginning." She turned looking back outside through the open doorway towards dad, though he was too far away for him to hear us. "And did you notice? But I think...dad had a woody!" she giggled slightly.

"We all did," I laughed back. "Just watching the three of you jogging along the beach, couldn't help it...none of us could. Why. That bother you that dad had a stiffy watching his wife and daughters?"

"No...not really, kind of naughty hot actually. Never seen dad's dick actually hard like that before. No wonder mom's always smiling. Though I daresay Brad...you could certainly give dad a run for his money in that department."

"Maybe him, but certainly not David. I'll say this for him, no wonder he has such good luck with the girls at school, that guys got a monster dick on him, even if I do say so myself."

"Oh? Didn't look like that much of a monster to me," she smiled, only then actually biting into her banana, chomping off half of it in response to that.

"You should have seen it last night," I grinned wickedly. "And then you'd know what I had meant by that."

"Something tells me...I must have missed something after you left," she grinned.

"You might could say that..." I said picking up a slice of cantaloupe, and then licking it in much the same way I had licked her last night.

"Do tell me," she grinned walking over, once more fondling my cock as the two of us stood there, dad just sitting a few feet away outside the door. Though we both noticed then, his hand was subtlety moving up and down in his lap as we stood there.

Standing there watching dad actually jerking himself off as I told her about the night before, all three of us just finishing as mom and Chris once more made an appearance just a short distance away down the beach again.

"Come on...let's go for a swim," I said taking her hand pulling her along behind me. "And besides, like you said earlier. You still owe me one."

**

We soon after made the short walk to the clear crystal pool, swimming for a time, even frolicking beneath the falls. Deciding to take a breather, dry off (amongst other things) we made our way up to the plateau from the other side, opposite of the way that Chris and I had climbed up. Once there however, we walked over to the exact same spot where Chris and I had been, spreading out a blanket to lie down on and allow the sun to dry us off.

"So...about time I returned the favor from last night isn't it?" Stacy said finally sitting up again, though I remained flat on my back, allowing her to basically shield the sunlight. At least in this way, I could look at her, watch her, as she sat beside me Indian style, already beginning to play and fondle with my rapidly growing dick.

She had barely even gotten started however when we both heard someone coming up the path that I had taken the day before.

"We've got company," I warned her, though she'd already heard it too, releasing my cock, though she made no effort to scoot away from where she'd been sitting. Slightly surprised, and somewhat relieved, it was Chris that suddenly emerged now walking...and smiling...towards us.

"Hope I didn't erupt...or better yet, miss anything," she announced walking over towards us, likewise placing her own towel and blanket down next to ours. The fact my cock spoke for us both said it all anyway, there was no sense denying it at this point.

"Actually...she was just getting started," I quipped smiling easily now, wondering in a way what might be expected next. Until I remembered that Stacy had no clue that it had been both Chris and I who'd been up here the day before. I figured it was best that I come clean with it before Chris said something.

"She saw us...well, me anyway...when we were up here watching the two of them yesterday," I announced. Only then Stacy realizing that I hadn't been alone up here.

"So...you saw us too then," she asked looking at her sister.

"Yeah, I did. And it looked pretty hot from where we were sitting," she added to that.

"Funny. I didn't see you sitting up here. Only Brad," Stacy said looking directly at me as she said that. "Where were you at the time?"

Now Chris was looking at me. "Probably laying down at that point," she said easily enough. "I dozed off after a while as cozy warm as it was."

I was grateful for the small omission. Pleased that Chris was wise enough to see that might, and could cause a small discomfort here if she was to actually tell Stacy what it was she had been doing at the time.

"Anyway...don't let me interrupt you," she said grinning now. "Besides, I'd like watching that myself."

"I ah...told Brad about us," Stacy said though she had already reached over taking my now VERY hard stiff cock in her hand again.

Chris laughed. "Figured you had, just a matter of time before I knew you would. No worries sis...it was going to come out at some point or another. Especially seeing you with Jessica yesterday. I figured if you hadn't told him about us yet, that you would...especially after seeing the two of you."

"You done anything with Jessica yourself?" I now asked, wondering just how many in the family she had been with.

"Not yet, never really had the opportunity or the inclination really. Not that I wouldn't given the chance mind you...but it's just never seemed to be the right time, or right place. Have you?"

Her question surprised me, though it made me chuckle as well. "No...I haven't, was almost starting to wonder why she hadn't approached me if she'd already approached everyone else. Though admittedly, she and I haven't gotten along any better than David and I have."

"Speaking of which," Chris said lowering her voice almost as though she was afraid of being overheard. "You should have heard the two of them going at it last night!"

"Jesus! You heard that?" I exclaimed, now suddenly worried, and wondering if anyone else had, if she had.

"Actually, I was still trying to go to sleep after everyone got back. Couldn't as yet though, still wired maybe from the club. Anyway...soon after, Jessica gets up, obviously sneaking out...so I followed her, and low and behold, she went straight over to David's hut. So I stood outside, watching them through the window."

I laughed.

"What?"

"So was I. Obviously on the other side. Didn't see you though," I snickered again, as was Stacy now, knowing the rest of the story. Now Chris laughed.

"So you mean to tell me you were watching them on one side, while I was watching them on the other one?"

"Apparently so," I laughed out loud again.

"Yeah, the only one still out cold and solidly asleep was this one here," Chris quipped looking at her sister. "You were out like a light!"

"That's because I'd already had my nice little orgasm...thanks to Brad here. Which is why I still sort of owe him one. Never did finish what I had started doing after we came back yesterday."

"Figured you two would," Chris confided. "I could see it in your eyes all during dinner, that you wanted to go back, and if you could manage it...that you'd prefer it if Brad came back with you. Obviously, everything must have worked out. Except for...that," she grinned again looking down at my still swollen, and now very purple aching cock as Stacy almost nonchalantly sat there flopping it about, playing with it. "Looks to me like it needs to cum. And like I said earlier...I'd very much enjoy watching that myself if neither of you too has any problem with it."

"I know I certainly don't," I informed them both. "And you're right...it really does need to cum here pretty badly too. It's been aching pretty much all day, especially watching you guys jogging earlier.

"For once, I have to say I wish I had your tits instead of mine sis," Stacy said cupping her breasts for a moment. "No more jogging for me without wearing support, that's for damn sure!"

"And I wish I had your tits," Chris told her, reaching over to now cup them herself, holding them in her hands. Stacy moaned as she did that, a reminder perhaps of past times together.

"Been a while since you've touched them," she stated, eyes closed, though her hand once more began stroking my now more than needful cock again.

"Yeah, it has been. And I've missed that. Tell you what. You finish off poor Brad here, as he obviously needs it. And afterwards, I'll treat you to something special, while he watches us. I'm sure he'll enjoy seeing that. How's that sound?"

I almost came then, just hearing her say that.

"It sounds...wonderful," Stacy sighed pleasurably, and then began working my cock up and down almost anxiously. "And how about you Brad? Think you'll enjoy seeing the two of us going down on one another?"

My answer came in the form of several white sticky eruptions that were soon filling the sky, and splashing almost everywhere and upon everyone seconds after hearing that.

**

Even though I had had one very fine, very intense orgasm, it didn't take long for me to be hard as a rock all over again. Just watching the two of them together was enough to do that. Seeing Chris and Stacy going down on one another simultaneously would have raised the dead.

They had both given each other multiple little orgasms by now, finally rolling away from one another, spent...exhausted, and thoroughly satisfied. The problem was, I of course was now ready again myself.

"Ah oh...look what we did," Chris laughed rolling over towards me. "Can't have him walking back looking like this now can we?" She asked her sister, as Stacy too now rolled over joining her sister as I stood there kneeling between the two of them.

"Certainly not," she agreed, and then as one, the two of them began licking and sucking me together.

The pure pleasure I now felt as their tongues and mouths at times became one, was too incredible for words. They licked, nipped, sucked, tickled, stroked and mouthed me to levels of ecstasy and enjoyment that I'd never experienced before. Once more hovering on the edge, Chris was the first to seemingly pick up on that.

"Ever tasted a man's cum before?" She asked Stacy.

"No, never had. Add that to the list of things I've never done with a man...yet," she hinted back. "But...I have wondered what that would be like."

"Keep going, you're about to find out," I informed them both, feeling my balls beginning to tingle with imminent release.

"Want to find out?" Chris asked again. "Because if not, it's ok...I'll be happy to take it," she told my sister.

"No...I want to, I really want to. And especially with Brad," she said honestly. "We'll take turns with it," she surmised, "You know...pass it back and forth to one another. You take a shot...and I'll take the next one."

"These aren't tequila shots here ya know," I said starting to grimace now, just barely managing to hold off here. "Not like I can control them after they begin."

"Here...we'll just place our mouth's close together, and you do all the work," Chris suggested. "Ready whenever you are," she then added as their tongues simultaneously went back to licking and flicking the tip of my cock again.

"Oh...I'm ready. More than," I said giving them final warning. "Because girls...here...it...CUMS!"

I knelt there, watching my cock explode. Ribbon after ribbon of spunk leaping from my prick tip. The girls almost fighting over it, tongues lapping, mouths sucking, and licking as Chris basically took over, grabbing my dick, feeding it to Stacy first, and then feeding herself, back and forth until they had each managed to suck out, draw out, and lick off the last remnants of my incredible spending.

"Well? What did you think?" Chris asked as I once more collapsed backwards, stars still filling my head at the moment.

"Salty maybe...but certainly nothing like I expected, or heard about. I quite liked it," she added to that. And then surprised me, and perhaps Chris too as she suddenly leaned forward kissing her sister, and thus sharing a bit of a cum-kiss with her as the two of them embraced, swapping spit, cum, and everything else again as it seemed.

"Alright you two, before you get all amorous and horny again, we'd best be getting back before mom and dad send out a search party for us."

We hurriedly gathered up our things after that, and began making our way down the hill back towards the huts. Now famished, we headed immediately over towards mom and dad's bungalow of course, especially as that's where all the food was. Neither one was there, and at first, nowhere in sight either.

"Maybe they went over to the resort," Stacy suggested.

"I doubt it. Unless they made arrangements to do so earlier or something. David and Jessica took the launch over this morning, not expected back until dinnertime. Dad already said he was planning to do a barbeque for everyone. So they must be around here somewhere."

I agreed with Chris. "Yeah...maybe they did go off looking for us though. Though the island isn't all that big. Not like you can really get lost here. Surprised we didn't run into them then, especially if they did come looking for us."

Just then, Stacy spotted the two of them out the window. "There they are...off a ways, down near the point there see? Just out in the water."

We all looked. Sure enough, it was them. Though as we continued to look, it was also obvious as to what they were doing too. Dad standing...mom on her back, legs locked around his waist, basically floating on the water as he obviously stood there fucking her.

"God, they're like a couple of horny kids aren't they?" Chris grinned, laughing. "I have to say, I'm not sure I've ever seen the two of them like this. Especially with their open-mindedness about not just them...but all of us running around in the all together out here. I don't think I've ever seen the two of them this horny before."

"I know what you mean," I said telling her about dad earlier this morning. Watching them jog, and then sitting there jacking off afterwards though Stacy and I were pretty sure he never realized we'd stood there watching him.

"I have an even better one for you," she then told us. "When we came back? Mom and I? You two had just left obviously, and as mom and I came running up towards dad, it was pretty obvious he'd just finished. There were little wet spots in the sand just beneath where he was sitting, but even better, he'd missed some. When we walked up, I teased him a little, but then so did mom if you want to know the truth, because she saw it too. She looked at dad, and honestly said, "So Bradly...getting off on your very own daughters are we?"

"She didn't!" I said laughing out loud.

"Oh yeah...she did! But that's not even the best part! Then she reaches down, swipes up a bit of his cream from the inside of his thigh and licks it from her finger, right there in front of me! And then says: Hmm, tasty as usual too!"

"Oh fuck! No shit! Really?" Stacy says laughing hysterically now.

"But even better..." Chris says again, once again lowering her voice conspiratorially, looking at the two of us. "And then I reached down, and swiped some of it off him myself, and then licked it off with the two of them looking at me, and said. "You're right mom...it is!"

"Oh my god! You didn't...did you? Really?"

"I did. I really, really did. Dad was a little stunned, just sitting there, until mom burst out laughing hysterically. Then she promptly sat down in his lap. Needless to say, I didn't stick around after that, but the look on his face was priceless. I'm willing to bet he fucked the shit out of mom right then and there after that. But by then of course...I'd gone looking for you two."

"You sure this place isn't called fantasy island?" I then asked. "Because I'm starting to think that everyone's most wickedly decadent fantasies are starting to be acted out here," I told them both. "I know mine certainly have been!"

"I'm half tempted to agree with you on that count," Chris stated. "And I'll tell you something else too that I found very interesting. I overheard mom and dad talking while we were waiting for the lunch to be made ready to bring us back. They had wandered off a bit, but you know how sound travels when you're next to the water, so I don't think they realized I could hear them as well as I did. Didn't get it all mind you, just bits and pieces here and there. But...what I did overhear them discussing was interesting enough. Dad said, and mom agreed with him, that while we're here. He said we, and mom agreed with him, that while we're ALL here, that whatever happens, no matter what...he's ok with. And mom said the same thing. The way they see it, this is a very, very special vacation, and one that we might never ever enjoy together again like this as they see it. Anyway...I then overheard mom telling dad, "But only if the kids are ok with it...agreed?" And then dad agreed to that, whatever that was."

"Wow...that IS interesting isn't it?" I wondered aloud. "Makes you sort of wonder what it was they were actually talking about doesn't it?"

"Well, I'll say this to that. We might find out tonight during the barbeque. Dad was very implicit about making sure David and Jessica were back in time for it. He told them, and me...that he wanted to have a little family chat during that time. And even said that he wanted us all to sort of dress up for the occasion. Apparently, they bought things for everyone and said that they'd be ready and waiting for us in our rooms prior to this evening."

"Maybe we should go see if they're there already then?" Stacy suggested curiously, to which we all agreed to, though I wandered back to the girls hut with them first before going back to my own place. Sure enough, there were tropical outfits sitting on their respective beds, though by the looks of it, they didn't look like anything more than a single wrap around floral print wrap of some sort as the girls held theirs up, inspecting them.

"Here's a note," Chris said as she began reading it. "In mom's hand writing. It says: Make something sexy fun out of this. Wear nothing else, and come to the barbeque with an open mind. Love, mom."

"Holy shit," I said wondering now, as the three of us quickly went back to my place. There was a similar package and note waiting for me as well. Another floral piece of cloth, but this one, much, much smaller. Barely enough to even wrap around myself. "You mean...this is it?" I asked still trying to figure out how I was supposed to wear the damn thing.

"That's it," Chris chuckled. "Here, it goes like this," she said fitting it around me, tying it off on one side. "There...just like that!"

"Shit, it's like wearing a skirt...or more like a mini skirt at that," I then added. "I might as well show up nude if this is all it is."

"I have a feeling, that's a lot closer to the truth here than any of us actually realizes. I have a feeling, this is apt to be, one very...very...interesting evening ahead of us."

I laughed again however looking at myself in the mirror.

"What?" The girls both asked.

"Well for one thing...imagine poor David trying to fit into something like this. As short as it is, I seriously doubt he'll have enough material to cover up that dangling cock of his!"

"Even better...what if it suddenly gets hard?" She then wondered.

And something told me, it would too. Especially with the girls standing around looking sexy in their outfits.

Once again the name "Fantasy Island" suddenly came to mind. I had other fantasies I hadn't told anyone about either. I mean after all, most men had them at one time or another. I certainly had. But I was beginning to wonder if they were a lot more feasible than I'd ever imagined.

We all three were now anxiously awaiting for the evening to come, and what else might actually be in store for us when it did.

I soon after heard the launch returning and knew that Jessica and David had likewise made it back in time as I returned to dress, the girls having gone back, no doubt doing the same.

I stood looking at my reflection in the mirror, already fighting my erection, trying to keep it down somewhat as I allowed certain thoughts to once more control my mind.

"Nah...no way," I finally said. And then headed out back to where I knew dad was already starting up the barbeque.

CHAPTER 2

By the looks of it, mom and dad had done a pretty good job of setting things up. Short of an actual Luau, it was going to be one hell of a feast. We were actually scheduled to attend a Luau in fact, sometime next week over on the main island. But for now, this was the next best thing. Dad was already starting steaks, though there'd be fresh fish as well. The girls had already set up tables with all sorts of delicately prepared side-dishes that the resort had done up for us. And though wearing a tropical print wrap similar to mine, dad's was considerably longer, making me wonder why mom had chosen much shorter ones for David and me. I didn't mind it too much however once getting it on, it was comfortable, and made me wonder briefly if this was sort of what it might have felt like wearing a Kilt. I might just as well been naked for all the support or coverage it provided me.

And yet, oddly enough, it would have felt really weird sitting down to eat with everyone being naked too. So I suppose wearing something at least seemed far more appropriate.

At dad's request, I moved some of the tables around just a little so that we'd all be able to sit down and eat together. As I finished doing that, mom came out with yet another tray of food along with some tablecloths to spread out. Almost immediately I saw what she had in mind when she said "make use of them in a sexy way." The floral print wrap she was wearing was a bright emerald green with various plants and flowers decorating it. But that wasn't what caught my eye. It was how she had chosen to wear it that did. She had secured it, tied it off so that it was worn mostly as a long dress reaching the ground. But one side was folded and tied up and over the shoulder, completely covering one breast, while fully exposing the other one. She looked sexy as hell in wearing it this way, and smiled briefly upon seeing me admiring the bold look.

"You like?"

I actually had to swallow before answering. "You look sexy as hell mom, admittedly, the one boob thing is kind of provocative." She laughed at that.

"Yeah, wearing it this way, I can show off my best tit, and tease with the other one."

"Best...tit?" I asked.

"Yeah," she giggled again now helping me as we spread out the tablecloth together. "They're not exactly the same size. This one's just a little bigger than the other one is. So this way, you really don't notice it so much."

To be honest, I'd never really noticed or found much, if any, of a difference between them. But then again, it was only recently that she'd been parading around fully naked too.

"I've never noticed a difference," I told her, hearing dad chuckle just behind me as I said that.

"That's because you probably weren't looking at them symmetrically," mom grinned, winking at me as she said that. "Though I hold you and your sister accountable for the difference. For whatever reason, you both seemed to prefer sucking on my left breast as opposed to my right one...try as I did."

"Me too!" Dad stated once again obviously listening in. "Just something about that left breast of yours," he said teasingly.

"Just be glad you men don't have to deal with something like that," mom chastised him back. "How'd you like it if you had one ball considerably larger than the other one, then you'd know how I feel."

I found myself actually standing there looking at my mother's bare breast. Seeing that I was, she easily released the still covered breast, now standing there directly in front of me. "See?"

I looked again, closely now. And yes, there was a small slight difference, but unless you actually tried looking for it, it was hardly even noticeable. "They both look good enough to me," I told her. "I think they're incredibly pretty in fact," I added to that, marveling at how firm and full they still were, hardly any real sag to them whatsoever, especially as firm and heavy as they really were. Perhaps not quite as high on her chest as Stacy, or Jessica's were. But given time, I knew that their breasts would perhaps droop even more so than mom's were.

"Thank you honey," mom said walking up to kiss me, and not on the cheek either. Kissing me on the lips. I honestly think her kiss, though still brief, lingered just a moment longer than what might have been usual. Enough at least that when we parted, her lips still seemed to pucker a bit as though still savoring the moment. But not only that, I had also felt the softness of her bare breasts pressed against my chest for that same moment. Her nipples, both now as it appeared, a bit harder, more pronounced than they had been a moment ago.

"Whew," I actually said, not realizing I'd voiced my feelings perhaps, though mom smiled almost seductively at me as she once more tucked away her breast back inside her sarong, recreating her original look.

"Go see what's keeping your brother," she told me. "See if he needs any help with his outfit."

"I think I'll see if Chris is up for doing that," I told her then. To which dad once more chuckled as he stood there turning the steaks.

"Send her in there to help...and they could end up missing dinner entirely!"

"Bradley!" Mom chortled, but then laughed as well. "Perhaps you're right...maybe I should go and see if he needs any help myself." With that, mom headed off towards David's hut, leaving me to stand there wondering about the comment dad had just made.

"How much had been going on anyway?" I wondered, "And more importantly, if it had...how much did they really know?" Somehow, I felt like we would learn a great many details this evening as the night wore on. But I was left to return to that thought later as my three gorgeous sisters finally came out at that moment, joining us.

Though the floral print patterns were basically identical in design, the colors were of course all different, as was the way the girls had chosen to wear them too. Jessica had adopted mom's idea basically, though BOTH of her breasts were bare, choosing to wear a bright red dress though it had been specifically picked out for her, with a white pattern, same as the others were. Though Stacy's was blue, and Chris's was actually a reverse of that, a white dress and black similar floral print. Jessica had worn hers as a full skirt, long to the ground, though she was completely naked from the waist up. Stacy was completely covered, but had used most of hers to wear her skirt very short, showing off a great deal of her perfectly shaped legs, though her breasts were teasingly encased in the rest of it, much like mom's one covered boob was. Chris was actually the more modest of them all, though she too had shortened her dress even more so than Stacy's was. Though I felt that my sister's perfectly formed ass really was her best feature, which she seemed to be showing off. I knew just looking at her, that her pussy was only inches away from being exposed, and no doubt would be if she were to bend over, or even in sitting down. Most of her dress was likewise covering her chest with a double fold over both shoulders, and was then tied off and secured on one side. Each in their own way did indeed look sexy as hell.

"About damn time!" Dad announced, though he too had been admiring his daughters just as I had been. We turned as one, as mom and David began making their way over towards us. David's short wrap, blue in color, where mine was black had been neatly formed and tied off along the side. It was clearly evident that his rather impressive looking tool was making an almost improper bulge just off to one side, making me feel for a brief moment, almost jealous at the obvious difference between us. Chris however, as usual, and almost as though reading my mind, leaned over whispering to me.

"Keep in mind honey...you're what I call a 'grower'. You start off small...er," she chuckled. "But...you grow considerably bigger. David pretty much stays the same size, just softer to harder is all. You've got nothing to complain about. Trust me."

Her words were both assuring, and yet once more alluded to the fact that she was a hell of a lot more aware of things that I obviously had been. And it again made me wonder, just who in this family had been doing what...to whom?

"Well, now that we're finally all here together, and while we're waiting for the steaks and fish to finish cooking, perhaps it's time we have that quick little family chat. But not before we enjoy a toast together, towards our time here, and this fabulous vacation we've all been enjoying." Dad and mom then began pouring each one of us what proved to be a very potent tropical drink of some sort. Dad even called it a "Tropical Island, iced tea," which to me, tasted like there was a bit of just about every kind of alcohol they had available inside the bar.

It was damn fucking good too. But I knew I'd have to go slowly with one, or two of these, or I'd find myself sucking pillow, instead of anything else later, which was my hopeful intent.

Mom's "good tit" coming to mind as I actually thought that.

**

After our family toast, dad began his brief speech to us all. "As you all know...yesterday, after arriving here, your mom and I made a point of letting you all know what our personal intentions were. We had already decided early on, that shortly after our arrival, we planned on showing you how truly uninhibited and carefree we really are. Especially away from those of whom might frown on it the society in which we live. At least here, we can be free to express ourselves as we see fit without judgment or recrimination. We both wanted you to see that, and experience that with us, to whatever extent or level you were all equally comfortable with. And...we were right. It didn't seem to take very long, that each one of you felt as comfortable and free as we did, in our respective nudities."

I noticed upon looking around that everyone was smiling, nodding their heads in full and complete agreement with him. So far...so good.

"And then of course...your mother and I," dad said winking at mom as he spoke, "took things to another level as well. Being intimate, openly, and affectionately with one another. We didn't hopefully, embarrass or do anything that seemed too flagrant, or too obvious. But the fact that I am sure most of you knew, we were being intimate, and enjoying one another, wasn't lost on any of you as to how we now approached doing that either. We are here after all...to have fun, relax, find enjoyment in whatever ways we feel comfortable doing."

As though they'd actually rehearsed all this, it was mom who now stood, as dad...as though on queue here, turned back to the barbeque, turning the steaks and checking on the fish to ensure it was cooking properly.

"We also wanted you all to know, we're not blind to things that have been going on in this family, as much as some of you might think we have been. Early on...when your dad and I first met, and long before we even got married. We talked about it. Talked about the difficulties of trying to merge different personalities and heritages into this family, not to mention then later...including two more of our own with Brad Junior, and Stacy. Obviously as you all know and remember, these were trying times, especially with times between David and Brad that for a long time, I didn't think would ever work out. Now at least...you two are civil to one another, so that's something at least," mom said looking at the two of us, as we in turn looked at one another, nodding heads.

"Your dad and I also discussed other things. Things that I know you were never fully aware of. Things we talked about, even planned for in a way, knowing the difficulties of trying to raise a ready-made family in one home. We knew going in...there would be curiosities, obstacles. Which we tried to manage as best we could, mostly by allowing each one of you to find your own way, work through those without either one of us having to step in until it was absolutely necessary. For the most part, I think that strategy worked. You all found your way, sometimes with one another, sometimes in confidences with each other that you didn't always share with anyone else...including your dad and I. The thing is, you did. But you also discovered some intimacy too. That was again something that was expected. We knew it would happen, it was virtually inevitable that it would. We didn't know in what combinations it might, or what the outcomes of such alliances would result in. Again...for the most part, I think things took their natural normal course. And obviously...since we've been here, that seems to have held true and continued on from there as well."

Once more, mom and dad seemed to exchange roles as he now began stacking the meat on a plate, which mom then carried over towards the table.

"Much as some of you might think otherwise, your mother and I weren't blind to some of the things that have been going on between some of you throughout the years. And...which I think I can easily say, have continued on here as well yes?" He asked looking at each one of us, though grinning now as he did that.

I almost chuckled at that, seeing several looks back and forth amongst everyone...me and Chris included in that, and to some extent...Stacy and I as well, though it was David and Jessica who seemed to be exchanging most of those looks between themselves.

"Hurry up Bradley," mom said interrupting him for the first time. "Before dinner gets cold."

Dad nodded his head, continuing. "So bottom line then is this...as far as we're concerned, though you are all our children, you're also all adults. And as adults, you are free to make your own decisions, seek your own desires and goals in life, whatever they might be...and with whomever they might be with. While we're here...especially here, your mom and I wanted you all to know..."

"That we're ok with whatever you want to do with one another," mom said jumping in again, obviously trying to speed things up a little here, though she quickly took it to another extreme, perhaps in getting more directly to the point. "If you want to fuck one another, feel free to do so. Even feel free to watch us doing it if you'd like...if something like that turns you on. I know...speaking for your father and I, we've enjoyed watching some of you, given the opportunity to do so that is."

I was a little surprised at mom's vulgar use of the word fuck, as she rarely used it. Just hearing the word, though I'd certainly said it enough times myself, seemed to escalate the overall mood and tone of this little family meeting we were having. Something I think we all felt and realized, especially when Jessica immediately spoke up taking advantage of that open door perhaps.

"You mean...you and daddy have seen me...seen us?" Jessica asked jumping in as well now, looking first at David, and then at Stacy, though that one I think, had somehow been missed by dad, up until now anyway, as he now looked over at her inquisitively. Though I also noticed, mom didn't.

"Once or twice," mom grinned. "Needless to say, we never questioned you about it now did we? Nor will we now either. All we are saying is this...if you choose to do so, especially while we're here, then feel free to do so. And that holds true for the rest of you as well," she then added. "Now...come, sit down, eat. We can talk about this further during dinner if you wish to. But lets not waist any more time and ruin dinner here by letting it get cold."

As we all stood and began heading over towards the carefully prepared table full of food, Chris was the first to make yet another comment, almost stopping everyone in their tracks.

"Daddy, you didn't say we were also having Polish sausage," she said looking serious. Though he looked at the barbeque for a moment as though half expecting to see some there, and then back towards her again, looking confused. "Either that...or a snake crawled up inside your wrap," she grinned, now pointing out the obvious. Dad's dick had risen just a bit, tenting out the front of it as he actually blushed, the rest of us looking, and then laughing a little at Chris's not too subtle awareness of dad's obvious arousal. She then looked at mom however, raising the question that I myself had been wondering about, and almost too afraid to actually ask.

"So does this mean if I wanted to, it would be ok for me to reach out and fondle dad's sausage if I wanted to?" She dared to ask mom.

Mom and dad glanced at one another, smiles on their faces. "This too is something we discussed, though we decided long before now, and agreed to again last night...it would be perfectly ok with us as well, as long as that none of you felt pressured, or obligated to do anything like that. We felt...as long as it was your desire, and not just our own, we'd leave something like that up to each one of you. But...since you raised the question, and asked it...let me say this. "It's up to you to let us know if that's something you want to do or experience. Neither your father nor I will approach any of you. So...that being said, let's eat, and let the rest of the evening more or less take care of itself. Everyone ok with that?"

I sat down next to mom, reached out, fondling her "covered" breast. "I think I need to make amends to this one," I said smiling at her. "If you'd let me," I then added to that.

"I'd like that. In fact...I'd enjoy that very, very much," she said similarly reaching over, her hand on my upper thigh briefly, and then quickly, far too quickly in fact, giving my now rock hard cock a gentle, affectionate squeeze through my wrap. I knew then, most likely before the night was over, I wouldn't be wearing it. Nor did I also have any doubt, most everyone else wouldn't be wearing their outfits any more either.

**

Not only was the dinner we were having together spectacular, but so was the mood and atmosphere now that everything had been literally and figuratively speaking...laid out on the table. Most everyone was laughing, even flirting with one another. The jokes getting more and more decadent, even some of the stories people began sharing, and then asking one another about.

"So mother...how many times did you and daddy catch David and I together anyway?"

Jessica curiously asked.

"A few times...twice for me at least, and I know for sure once with daddy," she answered. Though she also turned towards Stacy too. And once with you too honey," she smiled. "Though that time was with that girl-friend of yours, Dianna I believe? The girl you were sort of seeing for a while?"

Stacy seemed obviously surprised at that one. "You did? I mean, when...how, where were you?"

"One night when she'd come over for a sleep over as I remember. The two of you were down in the living room, sleeping together in sleeping bags? Remember that?" Obviously by the look on her face, she now did, though still somewhat bewildered by it. "Your daddy and I even fucked...watching you two, at the top of the stairs, though you never saw us of course. Somehow, we managed to keep quiet. I don't mind saying though...seeing you honey, was pretty erotic. I'm not sure how many girls you had actually been with by then, but it was certainly obvious, to me at least, that you knew what the hell you were doing, and that you obviously enjoyed doing it."

Stacy was blushing profusely now, especially glancing about at everyone else who sat looking...and yet smiling affectionately at her. Though she quickly turned the tables on mom at that point too. "So...have you ever been with another woman before mom?" She asked pointedly. And though mom hesitated for a moment, she quickly answered.

"Not really...no. I sort of experimented curiously when I was a lot younger yes. But I've yet to actually do much of anything with another woman. Not that I wouldn't, given the chance perhaps. But it just never really presented itself. No one I know at least would be into that. Not amongst the friends or people your dad and I know..."

"With the exception of Colleen," dad interjected. "More than once, she's hinted at that very possibility," he stated again.

"Well...with her maybe yes. But I'm not too fond of George, her husband, and you know damn well Bradley, one wouldn't come without the other."

"Literally speaking," he said causing everyone to laugh.

"Yes well, aside from Colleen..." mom said furrowing her eyebrows at dad, "aside from the little I did do when I was younger, I've never actually experienced being with another woman...no."

"So...you're saying you would then? Given the opportunity?" Jessica now asked furthering the interest in the question Stacy had posed.

Mom looked at her then. "Why? You offering?" Mom asked her back, just as pointedly now waiting on her response, almost longingly by the look in her eyes.

Jessica looked at Stacy. Stacy looked at Chris, Chris then looked at the two of them, and back at mom again.

"We are...if you're interested in finding out what that's like," Chris finished full circle here.

"Holy fucking shit!" David said, who had oddly enough been the most quiet and reserved all evening. Taking everything in of course, speaking rarely and only occasionally, certainly not boldly or vocally up until now. He happened to be standing at the moment too, having gone back over to the buffet table to load up his plate again, standing there dishing up, listening in, having heard this unexpected discussion taking place, and then blurting out the way that he had.

"Speaking of sausages," mom stated. We all sat looking towards David, each passing second now that we did, his wrap stretched in a certain specific place, causing him a great deal of discomfort by the looks of it. So much so, he actually put his plate down, looking at us, and then at himself again.

"Fuck this," he said, suddenly undoing the knot on the side, removing it. In seconds, his magnificent cock sprang free, sticking proud and straight out from his groin. I was actually smiling just a little. Chris had been right. He was a soft to hard kind of guy, where I was indeed a little too big one. Though his prick was indeed hard and stiff, it wasn't much bigger than mine was, once I too was hard. It had actually looked a lot bigger than it really was, maybe due to the light and shadows the way I had seen it. Regardless of that however, David had more or less just paved the way here for everyone else to begin doing the same.

"Here we go!" Dad said...emulating a recent commercial, which caused everyone at that point to burst out laughing.

**

Taking the time to digest our food a little, dad poured everyone another round of those stiff drinks, though at least by now, having food in my stomach would help. As dad walked over handing mom one, she surprised everyone, reaching up, undoing the makeshift belt on dad's wrap, pulling it away. Revealing when she did, his semi-rigid cock, which was the first time I had actually sat there looking at it. But then she surprised everyone even more, including dad as she playfully stroked it, coaxing it into hardness.

"Better...much, much better honey," she told him. "See girls? Like I said earlier, daddy has absolutely nothing to be ashamed of. And now you see why he manages to keep a smile on this old girls face."

"You're not old mother," I commented seeing her smile at the compliment. "Damn sexy in fact," I added to that, seeing her smile even more now.

Admittedly, dad had a nice looking dick, not quite as big as David's was perhaps, and maybe even mine...but it was certainly thick, and considerably hard as mom actually slapped it, making it spring downwards, and then up again, slapping against his belly. It was actually pretty hot and erotic, seeing her sitting there playing with him the way she was, right there in front of us. Her total lack of inhibitions at this point seemingly having an effect on everyone.

"Fuck mom...you could hang laundry on that!" Chris quipped, and then removed her wrap, actually piling it on dad's prick, which then Jessica did as well, followed by Stacy as she likewise removed hers. In moments, dad stood...his prick easily supporting the admittedly lightweight garments they'd all draped over him. But more importantly now...everyone except for mom was naked. I had removed my own wrap shortly after David had, proving my point in a sense, that I too had nothing to be ashamed of.

"Well...suddenly, I seem to be a bit overdressed here," mom said, and then simply seemed to shimmy out of her own gown as it fell down around her feet. Once more, our family stood together entirely naked, and obviously aroused in front of one another, with no awkward looks or hesitations as hands suddenly seemed to reach out here and there all at once. Chris once again seemingly leading the way here by her actions, dropping down to her knees in front of dad, one last time glancing upwards towards mom before doing anything. "Be my guest," mom answered the unasked question. "Your dads been fantasizing about that for years!"

I am willing to admit. Though I hadn't really given it much thought before now either, but seeing my very dear sweet sister, suddenly down on her knees, in front of dad, as she held his very hard cock in her hand, and then licking, sucking it. Was one of the most erotic things I had ever seen. My own cock was now aching for similar attention, though I was even more anxious to explore a few of my own hidden fantasies and thoughts with mom. I could see that was going to have to wait for a bit however, as Stacy and Jessica both led mom over to the table, which they had quickly cleared away. Now laying her down on it, I watched as the girls first began paying homage to mom's breasts, something I was envious and jealous of for a moment, though I was soon content, just as David now was, to stand there and watch this. We actually did find ourselves standing side by side, each of us no longer concerned, or even inhibited about standing there together like this, hard cocks sticking straight out in front of us.

"Who'd have thought?" he simply stated as we stood there looking on, watching Jessica as she nursed mom's right breast, and as Stacy once more seemed to take to the left one. I snickered at that quietly, looking forward to sometime soon...doing the very same thing myself.

Not to be left out however, and somewhat content for the moment anyway, dad nodded in mom's direction at what the other two girls were doing. Almost reluctantly, Chris removed dad's cock from her mouth, leaving it with a long drool-drip clinging to it as she did so. Even that looked decadent as all get out as dad sashayed over to where David and

I were standing. Soon after joining us, his sliver of mixed pre-cum and saliva, only then separating and landing down near his feet as we all stood there watching it.

"Plenty more where that came from," he proudly announced. "Though mom tells me...you're quite the load shooter Brad," dad grinned.

The girls were still nursing and sucking on mom's tits, mom's hands having now come up, cradling and cupping the two of them against her warmly, and affectionately. Chris just then reaching the three of them, and then moving up between moms legs, carefully bending them at the knee, even spreading her some as the three of us sort of side-stepped over just a little for a much better view of this.

"She did huh?" I answered, remembering...as mom had been the only other one besides Stacy to actually ever see me squirt. Chris too had caught me jerking off once, but never saw me actually come like Stacy and mom both had. And I remembered that, that particular instance had probably been the basis and foundation for some of my early on, masturbatory fantasies about mom after that. I remembered it as though it had happened yesterday.

"She actually saw you squirt?" David pressed.

"Yeah, she did," I found myself answering back, actually reliving the moment, relishing it, though seeing Chris as she bent forward now, actually starting to run her tongue up and down mom's juicy looking split was making me even hornier as I recalled that special moment in time, for both David and dad.

"Tell it Brad," Dad said urging me to do so, though I had every intention of doing just that. "Mom certainly told me the story more than once," Dad said to me, telling me in the instant that obviously it had had more of an impact on mom too than I knew at the time...or even now.

"That was the week that dad was away on business, I was still looking for a part time job, something to get by on while attending the local college nearby. Needless to say, I was at home...everyone else was supposedly out, leaving me home alone as it were. Mom had gone out shopping, with Colleen in fact now as I think about it. But anyway, for whatever reason, mom came home early, a lot earlier than was expected. I didn't even hear her come home, though at the time, I was pretty well into myself at that moment. But worse, I was doing it in a place I probably shouldn't have been doing it either..."

"Where?" David asked, though our eyes all currently remained glued on the four women who were quite obviously enjoying themselves. I laughed though, interrupted for the moment when even mom spoke up, though she spoke in clipped, panting words as she did.

"Don't...leave...anything...out...either!" she spoke, the lustfulness in her tone of voice readily apparent. "It was very...hot," she added to that with a very deep moan, as Chris suddenly seemed to draw mom's hard little clit even more deeply into her mouth, sucking it.

"I was in her bedroom," I began again, surprised mom was still listening, once more obviously enjoying this moment, which seemed to be adding to the pleasure her daughters where bringing her. Which pleased me some as I continued on, now anxious if anything, to completely tell the story, and not leave out any details as I may have done a few moments ago. This was for her now...more than anyone, and I could have cared less what any of them might have thought upon hearing it. "Where I obviously had no real business being. But the thing was...I was horny, obviously...and unbeknownst to anyone at the time, I'd gone into mom's room with a purpose. I had rummaged through her dirty clothes hamper, found what I had hoped to find...which was a pair of her soiled panties. Admittedly, I was in a very dirty...horny mood. And as such, I wanted something dirty to use while I pleasured myself. So I rummaged around until I found a pair of mom's panties, which I was currently using to stroke myself off with. There... in her bathroom. Needless to say, I hadn't heard her, though in defense of that, when she saw me standing there, and realized what I was doing...she didn't say anything either, and continued watching me. I was right on the verge, hovering on the edge. Already the sensation of my balls getting ready to release when I felt...more than anything, an awareness of someone there behind me. I turned, still stroking my dick with mom's panties of course, and there she was, standing in the doorway of the bathroom, watching me. But even more than that, she had her hand down the front of her pants at the time. I didn't see anything obviously, but it was evident she too was now fingering herself. That was all it took, that triggered it. I couldn't have stopped it then if I had tried to. Suddenly I was squirting...spurting, my semen literally shooting out towards her. As though in slow motion, I watched it hitting her, I watched it as it soaked the front of the white blouse she was wearing..."

Mom's moans were deeper now, throaty as she began to pant, still listening. I walked over closer towards her, now stroking my dick, telling the story...dad and David both soon joining me as we all gathered around now, David too stroking, as was dad...all three of us uninhibitedly playing with ourselves in front of everyone, mom looking up now...seeing us, her "cum-face" already starting to make an appearance. Even Jessica and Stacy had quit sucking her breasts, though still holding them, kneading them, pinching mom's nipples. Only Chris continued on, still chewing and gently sucking on mom's hard precious clit.

"I couldn't believe the volume...bigger than any I had ever had before. Squirt after squirt continued to erupt from my prick. Mom still standing there, still fingering herself, watching me...watching my dick as I emptied myself all over the front of her. And me...using her very own panties to be doing it with! Mom came...just as I managed to milk out the very last half decent discharge against her, and then came over to me, hugging me...kissing me on the lips. I could feel the wet sticky mess now clinging to the two of us, my spent cock digging into her tummy. It was one of the best orgasms of my entire life!"

Mom cried out then in extreme ecstasy. Her orgasm just then claiming her, washing over her. And as she did that...I looked down, not at all surprised to see the cum once more leaping from the end of my dick. I saw it soar over my sister's head, splashing against my mother's stomach and breasts, and then as Chris finally did raise up a little, more than one spurt actually catching Chris in the back of the head.

But I wasn't the only one.

No sooner had I finished tossing off my load, I saw another racing by me, and like my own, this one likewise splashing against mom too, lower down this time, nailing her upper thigh, though Chris had turned at this point, immediately opening her mouth, dad's third and forth jettison of cream suddenly being claimed there. David joining us...Dad still squirting, me now milking...dripping out what was left, which I now smeared against mom's still lovely, still somewhat neglected imperfect breast, as David stepped up to the plate and proceeded to drench both of mom's breasts in his own joyous, over abundance of cum-cream, nearly as voluminous as my own.

No one spoke for several moments after that. Only the sound of excited breathing filling the air.

Finally dad did. "Well, I don't mind telling everyone, especially now. Up until mom told me about what happened, I had never once entertained the idea of doing that myself. I am now proud to say however, since then...I've done so several times. And I have enjoyed jerking myself off, with each and every one of the girls...dirty, soiled...cum filled panties!"

"Daddy! You dirty...dirty old man you!" Jessica grinned, and then promptly came over and began licking his spent dick clean.

David stumbled back against the table sitting down. "Well damn...obviously, I've been missing out!" He said, as everyone laughed.

"I think I've got a pair here with me you can use if you'd like to find out," Chris informed him. "Or I'd be happy to do it for you if you'd like me to," she then added to that. David sat, smiling nodding his head, already his cock seemed to bounce just a little rather than just laying there looking like a dead snake. Mom finally strong enough to roll off the table then, still looking quite the sight.

"Well...that was a nice way to begin the evening," mom stated finally sitting up, cum dripping and running everywhere it seemed as she did that. "In the meantime...I think we all need another drink...and then I believe, it's someone else's turn here on the table. Though by the looks of it...I'd say your father won't take too long to get ready again. Not with the way Jessica's sucking his cock!"

She was right too. And obviously my sister was enjoying every minute of it as she knelt there in front of him, doing that.

**

We did take a bit of a breather then though, freshening drinks, though I opted for a glass of wine instead of another one of those almost too stiff tropical drinks mom had made. My head was swimming enough as it was from all the excitement, not to mention the recent incredible spending I'd just enjoyed.

"So...I'm curious mom," Stacy now asked as we sat still trying to collect ourselves, though Jessica continued to sit next to dad at the table, still fondling and toying with his now once again hard cock.

"Yes dear?" Mom replied.

"After you caught Brad jerking off in your panties, and especially as he basically saw you masturbating too in a way...while you did that. Nothing else ever happened then after that?"

"Surprisingly no...it didn't. I think we were both too shocked afterwards in realizing that we'd actually enjoyed it. Brad was indeed a bit embarrassed at first, hardly even looking me in the eye after that for the first couple of days. But it was then that your father came up with the perfect solution, that seemed to settle everything, though again...nothing else ever happened between us."

"And what was that?"

I spoke up, answering that question myself. "Two days later, I came into my room, saw that mom had tucked a pair of her recently worn panties just under my pillow. I knew then that what had happened, was perfectly all right, and that mom didn't have any problems, concerns or worries with regards to my having done that. Periodically after that, I'd find another pair waiting for me. So it became a bit of an intimate little game between us. I'd use her panties to jerk off into, and then return them soon after back to her room."

"Where I on the other hand, would then take them, after Brad had cum in them, and use them on myself to masturbate with," mom stated once more surprising everyone with this intimate little revelation we'd just shared. Though dad obviously, knew all about it. Something that up until now, I hadn't known.

"And here I thought we were bad!" Jessica spoke obviously surprised upon hearing this, as she looked towards David.

"You were bad...and it was fun watching you," dad said in response to that. "You have no idea the number of times I had wanted to tell you that, approach you. But as your mother and I long ago agreed, that unless you approached us first...we never would. Until now anyway."

"Come on then...dad," Jessica said wickedly, pulling him by the cock towards the table. "I think it's about time you and I indulged ourselves then...don't you?" She then turned towards her sisters as dad climbed up onto the table. "Come on girls...come join us. Only fair after the attention we all gave mom, that we do the same for daddy too don't you think?" Only Stacy hesitated, not because she wasn't interested, or aroused...but she seemed nervous as to what might now be asked or expected of her. Once again mom came to her rescue however, speaking up.

"Stacy's still a virgin," mom said..."In the technical sense anyway," she added to that. "I'm not sure she's ready to go much beyond what she already has, so let's not place her in a position of doing anything more than that. Why don't you ride your father's prick Jess...since that was the original intent anyway, and let your other sister's do whatever it is they're comfortable in doing."

Jessica now straddled dad in a reverse cowgirl position, with his legs dangling over the edge of the table. Seeing that, Stacy made the quick choice to stand between him there, her intent and desire obvious as she waited briefly for her sister to slide down over our father's cock...fucking him, before leaning inwards. She was soon licking, teasing and mouthing the two of them while they fucked. Chris quickly seized the moment, climbing up onto dad's face, facing the other way, back to back now with Jessica. Here she presented dad with her wet juicy split, which he immediately began tonguing and licking.

"Well now...I guess that leaves the three of us doesn't it?" Mom stated. "Come here boys," she said suggestively. "Let mommy have some fun with the two of you."

At first unsure as to what she had in mind, and though no longer squeamish, or being at odds with David, I couldn't help wondering what she was up to. It didn't take long to find out. Having us stand there together on either side of her as she sat on the bench seat of the buffet table. She quickly reached out, taking us both in hand, and then drew us together, forcing us to step even closer to her, and one another. David and I for the very first time ever, now stood cock-tip to cock-tip, mom's mouth surrounding us both to some extent, as she began licking and sucking the two of us simultaneously. It felt heavenly, and surprisingly enough, looked erotic as hell too...watching mom's tongue snaking out, licking the two of us, seeing it circling our respective cock heads as her tongue danced and flicked our pricks. The feel of mom's mouth on me, and I am sure as David felt it too, sent a cascade of goose bumps up and down my spine. I reached down, finding one of mom's breasts, pleased that it was her "so-called" neglected one, and began toying with it. David too soon did the same, the two of us now fondling mom's tits while she continued to mouth, suck and lick us together, even teasing us, in a weird sort of way, as she periodically rubbed the head of our dicks back and forth against one another, amusing herself.

I don't think either one of us minded her doing that however, as it was her hands wrapped around us, doing all the teasing and toying, though she now began taking turns with each of us, more fully sucking and exploring us individually with her mouth.

It was also very nice, having mom doing that, while standing there looking over towards dad and the girls. Jessica was obviously enjoying herself, riding dad's dick, slowly working herself up and down, while Stacy in turn, took turns...though it was hard to see much from my vantage point, licking the two of them. Chris however was contentedly riding dad's face, his hand up, cupping and playing with her cute perky breasts. It was easy to see his fingers as they held, pinched and pulled on my sister's hard nipples, something I now knew she took a great deal of delight in, while having them played with in this way.

"Oh god daddy...I need to warn you," she said suddenly, her face already starting to screw up in a pleasured grimace. "I tend to get...very liquid down there whenever anyone eats me like this," she said pleasurably. To which dad merely grunted, still licking, if not even more so now upon hearing her say that.

Even mom looked up having heard that, though she maintained the two of us within her hands, still stroking our cocks, even rubbing them against one another again. "Like mother, like daughter," mom said. "I tend to do that as well whenever I'm having my pussy eaten too," she told us.

Only seconds after that, poor dad was drowning in a flood of cascading pussy juice as he fought to drink it all, lapping away at my sister's cunt, Chris crying out into the night as her orgasm claimed her. Jessica too seemed to suddenly hit hers as well only moments after that. Perhaps the effect of hearing Chris juice, her cry of ecstasy, the gurgling climax as dad drank from his daughter's pussy. Though I am sure it helped a lot that Stacy was at that very moment, sucking on Jessica's clit for all she was worth too.

"Fill me daddy...fill me!" Jessica called out now in the throes of her own climax. Though the way dad suddenly rose up, almost lifting Jessica off the table completely, it appeared as though he was at that very moment...doing just that. Pouring his own seed deep into the depths of my half-sister's womb.

"Oh man...fuck...mom!" David's clipped words announced. Turning just then as mom gathered him fully into her mouth again, stroking his cock, yet somehow still holding onto my own as she took him. I saw her cheeks suddenly expand, saw David go weak in the knees for a moment as he began spurting off into mom's mouth. Somehow she stayed with it though, swallowing, sucking...draining my brother's balls until once more he stepped back, collapsing down on the bench seat sitting next to her. She then turned towards me, eyes smiling, her mouth still full of cum as she finished swallowing, and then licking her lips.

"Hmm, yummy. But now I'm thirsty for a lot more...whenever you're ready baby. Mommy wants your cream!"

As mom cupped and held my balls, caressing them, she soon went back to sucking the head of my dick, paying particular attention to it, though gently stroking me at the same time. It wasn't long after that I felt the surge as it began to make its way up my shaft, just when I glanced over and saw Stacy now standing beside me looking on. I reached out, cupping my sister's breast, she smiled, drew closer to me, and then reached down replacing mom's hand with her own...jacking me. The moment she did that, I came...massively, spurting off into mom's mouth as she sucked, trying desperately to swallow the deluge of semen I began pouring forth. Unsuccessfully however, as a great deal of it soon appeared at the corners of her mouth and dripped down obscenely, onto her breasts.

I thought it looked cool though...seeing that. Especially when moments later, Stacy leaned over and gently began cleaning mom's breasts off with her mouth.

**

We were all pretty well drained, exhausted...spent. Slowly drifting off to our own bungalows for some much needed sleep. The fact that we hadn't done much more than we had, or even with others, held promise for the days ahead. We'd been on the island for a little over two full days now...and considering everything that had happened already, I knew now we had barely scratched the surface of what lay ahead.

I was just drifting off to sleep when I suddenly felt Stacy slipping into bed next to me, snuggling up behind me, spooning me instead of me spooning her. It felt nice...comfortable, perfect. Though even as she did that, I realized that she hadn't really gotten off, though certainly helping in the efforts to see to it everyone else did. I was about to offer, and suggest doing that for her myself when she spoke in a sleepy tone of voice.

"Eat me up in the morning," she said already sounding like she was drifting off to sleep as she said it.

"What?"

"Don't wake me up...eat me up," she sighed happily, pressing herself even more firmly against me from behind as I then heard the soft gentle sounds of her breathing steady out with contented sleep.

I was already looking forward to the sunrise.

CHAPTER 3

As promised, I ate her up twice. Waking to the warmth of the morning sun as it tossed a warm blanket of light over the two of us. Stacy still snuggled up close to me, her steady breathing and gentle snoring confirming the fact she was still sound asleep. I carefully pulled away, but in doing so...managed to nudge her more fully onto her back. With the two of us already being nude, it was an easy matter to likewise tenderly spread her legs, crawling up between them. I took the time to truly appreciate the beauty of my sister at this point, unhurried, gentle...relaxing in a very unique, sensual way.

Stacy moaned softly in her sleep. I waited for a moment, ensuring she had drifted off into a deeper sleep once more before continuing. I wanted this to be dream-like in a way, if I could manage it. Plus...I was truly enjoying myself too. As lightly as I could, I ran my fingertips up through the folds of her pussy, watching them suddenly spread like a flower opening in the morning sunlight. She was already moist, reminding me again of the morning dew still clinging to the petals of her delicate flower, as I felt the pearly-like slickness against my fingertip. I placed my finger against my lips, savoring her taste. Once more she sighed contentedly as I did that, yet still asleep. I waited a moment more, and then gently eased forward, running the flat of my tongue up the entire length of her precious slit. I did so as lightly, and as slowly as was possible, stopping short at the apex of her still somewhat hidden clit. I retreated back the other way, once more plowing the furrow of her sex with my tongue, this time allowing it to probe a bit deeper, yet soft, slow as I did so. She again moaned in her sleep, stirring just a bit as I again stopped, waiting.

Already her lips were beginning to swell. Walking my fingers back up to the top of my sister's cunt, I gently nudged the protective hood from her clitoris, watching it as it emerged. It too changing color, stiffening, and hardening like a miniature cock. The precious glistening head of her pink clit seeming to pulsate as I allowed my finger to dance on the surface of its glistening little clit-head. Stacy moaned again, once more stirring, and I knew that much more of this, she would slowly begin to wake. For now at least, she appeared to be dreaming, that early morning realm of reality and dream state, where one seems as real, as substantial as the other. I ran my tongue upwards again, this time however, flicking softly at her clit, fingers once more spreading, revealing. I kissed it, kissed it again, a gentle soft lingering suck before turning once more down her now even wetter split. The taste and aroma of her juices now assailing my senses. I probed, tongue-fucked, lingered with quick butterfly flicks of the tongue against her clit again. Like a fighter at the bag, the tempo and speed ever increasing, but only until she stirred again, her breath suddenly changing...did I then slow again. I felt her relax, ever so close to opening her eyes, allowing her to drift off once more. My breath hot against her quim, soft whispers of desire caressing the throbbing, pulsating stem of her sweetness until she once more seemed to sink back into the bed. I smiled outwardly, and inwardly, once more beginning the silent torture of her sex. This time running a single finger in through the wet, succulent opening of her sex, feeling the warmth of her essence now coating it, securing it, and likewise now throbbing and clasping about it.

"Ohhh," she moaned once more. This time forming words as wakefulness began to approach. With one finger inside, gently caressing, petting her, I now took her hard little nubbin firmly between my lips and began sucking it, though still as gently as I could. All the while looking upwards now, seeing the flutter of her eyes as they fought for consciousness.

"Almost there...almost there," I thought. I could tell by the response of her body, and by the way that her juices were almost free-flowing now, that she was a lot closer to orgasm than her conscious mind realized. Once more I felt her pussy clamp down tightly on my finger. I felt the increase and intensity of her inner muscles as they throbbed in spasmodic release, accompanied by a sudden surge of liquid sweetness. Her eyes fluttered open, for a moment looking bewildered and confused. My lips only then drawing in her clit fully, sucking it firmly, holding...sucking...seeing recognition, and just as suddenly rapture as her eyes closed once more.

"Oh my god!" She cried out, and then simply succumbed.

Even before she had fully come down from her climax, I allowed her the grace of working through her super-sensitivity. Feeling her relax, her breath still coming in gradual gasps however as she gathered herself. I renewed the earlier assault on her now very awake pussy and soul.

"Oh god...oh fuck, yes...yes Brad. Eat me! Eat me! Eat me!"

**

"Come on you two...get a move on," mom said standing in the open doorway of my bungalow. Any other time, she would have given us start, but not this time. That simple morning greeting telling us both in an instant, just how much things had changed. She stood smiling, not at all alarmed or worried about seeing the two of us together, though all we were doing was laying there at the moment, Stacy...still basking in the afterglow of her second very intense orgasm.

"That's right," I said remembering.

"Yeah, they'll be here within the hour," mom said once again. "So you two really should get something to eat before we go." She turned preparing to leave, but then suddenly stepped back into the room again, crossing over towards the bed where she leaned over, kissing the two of us affectionately. "There'll be time for more of that later," she grinned, winking at the two of us, and then departed.

It was odd seeing mom standing there wearing a somewhat modest, white two piece swimming suit. But it was a subtle reminder of what had been planned for the day. Weeks before the trip, we had all gone out and gotten certified to scuba dive, including mom, though she'd been initially reluctant in the beginning to do so. Ironically, perhaps more than anyone else, she had taken to it quite naturally, and thoroughly enjoyed herself while getting used to breathing underwater. She was the first amongst all of us to qualify, and was now looking forward to this private little excursion out in the reefs, more so than anyone else.

Stacy and I quickly dressed, soon joining the rest of the family for a quick bite to eat. Everyone anxious and excited now to actually practice our diving skills in the clear, crystal blue water near someplace called "The fish bowl". We had already been made aware, that this was a "clothing optional" dive, as had anyone else who'd be joining us on the trip. And though we initially started out dressed in swimwear, once underway...everyone was then free to remove their clothing if they then chose to do so. A short time later, a very large catamaran approached our small little island. We then waded out, boarding the boat, where our rented gear was already waiting for us. Besides the seven of us, there were only two other couples, likewise friends, as it appeared who had booked the same excursion. Introductions were soon made all around. Bill and Barbra Matthews were a young attractive looking couple, mid thirties perhaps, along with John and Jill Stevens. We laughed as they told us to refer to them as BB and JJ, something both couples actually answered to, as they explained the unplanned unions of their respected first names all starting with the same letters. David looked at me, and by the expression on his face, I could see he was dying to tell them about my name. Thankfully, refraining from doing so. Indeed, much really had changed between us, only weeks ago...he'd have taken delight in trying to embarrass me with such a comment.

As we headed out to sea, and towards the "fish bowl", it became obvious that realizing we were indeed a family traveling on vacation together, that there might be some hesitancy on our part to accept nudity around one another.

"Will any of you have a problem if we remove our clothing for the dive?" Barbra asked. "It's one of the reasons we booked this trip," she said inquisitively to that.

"Same reason we did," mom spoke surprising her a bit as Barbra and Jill both, once more took in the seven of us, wondering perhaps. "No worries...we're nudists," mom added to that, as though that perfectly explained everything to them. I saw dad hiding a sly smile upon hearing that. But the other two women smiled then, nodding their heads in acceptance and understanding, more importantly, reaching around and almost immediately undoing the bikini tops they'd been wearing. The moment they began doing so, everyone else did as well. Dad eyeballing the new scenery briefly, and his whispered comment once more reflective of what he's said the day before when we'd truly started getting familiar with one another.

"Here we go...again!" He grinned.

I noticed as soon as the bikini tops came off the other two women, that neither one of them was any bigger than Chris was. Chris in fact seemed rather delighted in that herself, suddenly no longer having the smallest breasts there. In seconds however, everyone was once again naked as we slipped into our diving gear in preparation for the dive. Listening to last minute instructions from the diving instructor and guide, everyone was instructed to buddy up in two's or threes, and ensure that they remained in constant contact with one another. The water was once again crystal clear, and the visibility near perfect. We'd also be diving in less than fifty feet of water, with the spectacular view of the coral reef below us, and a wide variety of colorful fish all swimming about. I was paired up with mom. Stacy...Chris both joining dad, leaving David and Jessica together, which everyone had pretty much expected them to do. We soon entered the water, and then began heading off in differing directions taking in the sites along the reef. There were various outcroppings of rocks and ledges, which concealed a wide variety of fish, though cautioned about going too deeply into any of those crevices, because of electric eels possibly being hidden within those areas.

Though we could see others a short distance away from us, like us...everyone seemed to be preoccupied with their own explorations, basically just keeping an eye on one another and not too concerned about where everyone else was. The sensation of weightlessness was in and of itself intoxicating in a way. But so was seeing mom swimming nearby, the total freedom of movement that she had, not to mention the way her breasts seemed to move so alluringly as she did that. Before I even realized it, I was hard, swimming beside her with a full out erection, something that didn't go unnoticed for very long. We had just then gone around one corner of an outcropping of rock, barely out of sight from any of the others. As though planned, mom came towards me, her hand immediately coming out to surround my cock. We sat there, our feet kicking just enough to keep us both virtually motionless, my own hands now cupping and caressing her breasts. It was eerily erotic, looking into one another's eyes through our masks, unable to speak, and yet saying so much merely by looking at one another. It took no effort at all. Reaching around behind her, my hands now on my mother's ass, I easily lifted her upwards. She came to me, her legs spreading obscenely as she did, fitting herself perfectly around and about me. We continued to float there together, the head of my prick nudging the opening of her sex, which she soon gathered into herself. For the first time ever, I felt the head of my prick suddenly engulfed in the surprisingly slick, slippery passage of her womanhood, the very place that I had myself once come from. I entered her inch by inch, savoring the excitement of this so taboo coupling until I was buried to the hilt inside my mother's cunt. In a sensual dance of pure weightlessness and control, we rolled, turned, twisted, all the while fucking one another so uninhibitedly, so effortlessly.

Finally at one point, I looked out to the side, realizing in our unbridled dance, that we had reemerged from the safety of our little enclosure, now fucking far more openly where we could so easily be seen. I needn't have worried however, for we weren't the only ones. Though I briefly felt concern as only a few yards away, Bill and Barbra, likewise engaged... coupling just as we were, glanced over, watching the two of us as we in turn fucked...watching the two of them. There was no hiding the fact now...which they now had to know, I was indeed fucking my own mother!

And...more importantly, I was too far gone to care at the moment either. The exquisite sensation of actually being inside her, soon had me quivering from head to toe inside. I felt the bubbling rush of semen racing up the length of my shaft, I felt it begin to pulse, squirt, and leap from my cock, filling my mother's womb. She in turn, thrusting, humping and grinding against me in equal and obvious ecstasy.

We soon after parted, both pleasured and satisfied in search of other members of our group. It was an interesting spectacle coming upon dad. Stacy floating on one side of him, Chris on the other. Each one with their hands on his prick, jerking him off. Just as we arrived, within mere feet of them now, mom and I watched as his prick began to jettison milky white clouds of semen that quickly spread out in all directions at once, much to everyone's amusement. Chris and Stacy both made feeble attempts at chasing it, capturing it, though continuing to milk out as much of it as they possibly could from dad's prick.

I soon after spotted David and Jessica, who had surprisingly...actually hooked up with John and Jill. It was like watching an underwater, choreographed ballet. Jessica's hands outstretched holding onto Jill's, David behind Jessica, John behind Jill, fucking them almost, but not quite, doggy style, letting the buoyancy of the water and the girls steering them to keep them so easily positioned as they sat there floating, fucking respectively, watching one another. Seeing this, I found myself becoming aroused again, just as Stacy came swimming up next to us. I was surprised when she removed her mouthpiece, slinking down in front of me. In moments, she had gathered my hard stiff cock into her mouth, and began to expertly, suck me off...right there under the water!

As surprised I was at this, I was even more surprised when mom soon joined her. The two of them now taking turns, one breathing air, the other sucking, though the way they managed to do it, there was hardly any disruption at all as the two of them together quickly brought me towards yet another, hard-felt, first ever...underwater blowjob.

As interesting as it had been to see dad's prick squirting...or rather 'clouding' as it where...under water, it was even more so...seeing my sister's mouth, and mother's too...opening as that same milky-white cum-cloud emerged from both, almost as though blowing smoke out in a way, the way that it escaped from their mouth's and lips, drifting upwards before each one reinserted their respective breathers again.

Unfortunately our time was up, so we began making our way back to the boat, soon climbing aboard. At first, the chat and banter was about all the beautiful sites we had seen, the colorful fish swimming about, though it was John who then purposely changed things in a differing direction.

"That wasn't the most amazing, or even beautiful sight I was admiring," he began. "Watching all that hot underwater sex taking place was what was really and truly beautiful!"

I had at first been fearful, wondering what they would think. Obviously they had seen mother and I together, and John and Jill had in fact actually been with David and Jessica in a way, so it was quickly and clearly obvious that we had a very incestuous family here.

"And time we came clean too," Barbra said saddling up next to mom, actually putting her arm around my mother's waist. "We're not just friends," she began to explain. "Jill is in fact my sister-in-law. She's the one who is married to Bill, my brother. John is in fact Jill's brother, who is likewise married to me. So...now you know a lot more about the four of us too."

It soon came to light that the four of them had been traveling about, vacationing for years in this way. Basically switching partners for the duration of their vacations together, though certainly enjoying the combined company of one another as well, sleeping in the same rooms together, rather than separate, truly making the most of it.

"Kind of nice being able to share that with someone, rather than hiding who and what we are all the time," Jill added to that, smiling provocatively towards David and Jessica, who stood smiling and grinning back at her once the full story came out.

"Yes...it is," Jessica said. "This vacation for us, has been an eye-opening experience as well, and one that was long overdue I think."

We soon retired to enjoy lunch, now sharing stories and experiences with one another, taking advantage of the beautiful calm seas as the boat sailed along smoothly. With the Captain and his two-woman crew fully approving of our 'on deck' dalliances, it wasn't long before everyone was locating and picking a spot, to pick up where we'd all left off earlier below the waves.

But I think I was even more surprised, when Barbra saddled up to mom there on the open deck, at first asking if she'd like for her to put some suntan oil on her back, which she began doing. Though it wasn't long before it looked a lot more like caressing, than applying oil to her. I then saw her whisper something into mom's ear, as mom then looked up towards dad who sat next to the two of them looking on. His erection clearly showing as he sat admiring everything going on about him, though in particular...mom and now Barbra.

"Feel free," dad told her. "We're on vacation here...so why not? As long as we're all consenting of course," he added to that. Mom nodded her head in agreement with that, as Barbra quickly took advantage, slithering down between mom's outstretched legs, and almost languishly, began going down on her. That simple act seemed to open an entirely different door. The moment Barbra and mom started up together, Jill too came over to dad, soon sitting in his lap as the two of them began to almost too causally fuck. John had actually approached Stacy, though she politely declined, seeking refuge perhaps by coming over to sit next to me, though Jessica quickly offered herself up, much to John's delight as Jessica now stood up leaning against the rail, John behind her, thrusting away.

Stacy immediately crawled up into my lap. And for a moment, I actually thought her intent was to fuck me, astonishing as that was. Seeing the surprised look in my face however, she merely winked at me, whispering. "Not quite ready for that yet. Though if I was going to fuck anyone...I think it really would be you Brad," she told me. "But until then...how about, just rubbing against me, while I rub against you. Would that be ok?"

"More than!" I assured her, as we began doing just that, though I even think mom thought we were doing it as she glanced over towards us, now grinning from ear to ear.

With everyone else fairly engaged, that left the final pairing up to being Chris and Bill of course, which just seemed to work out quite naturally. Laying down on the deck, almost right beside mom, Bill now began sliding in and out of my older sister, while Chris joyfully sucked on one of mom's breasts as Barbra's rapidly flicking tongue delighted mom elsewhere.

"Well, I'll say this much," Stacy said hugging me even closer to her now, pressing her soft warm breasts against my chest, her slick, slippery cunt riding up and down, sliding against my cock, though I was sorely tempted to impale her on it. "This is one vacation we'll not soon forget."

"You can say that again sis," I agreed with her, though I quickly took her face within my hands looking at her deeply, just before kissing her unlike I had ever kissed her before. "But I'll add this to that too...I hope sis, that even when this vacation comes to an end...that we won't."

She looked at me, though rather than saying anything, she simply pressed herself even harder against me, and for a moment, making me wonder and think if she wasn't half tempted to impale herself on me right there and then...though she didn't. But what we did do...was then kiss one another, unlike any way we had ever done before. And we both came...right in the middle of doing that.

**

The sun was just beginning to set when we pulled back into the resort. It had been a long, but very pleasurable and adventurous day. Once again however, everyone was tired, and more than ready to call it an early night. I sure as hell knew I was, exciting as it had been, I was in dire need of sleep at this point. Though by the looks of it...so was everyone else. As we stood waiting for the resort launch to take us back over to our own cozy little island, I saw the girls suddenly gather a short distance away, conversing in hushed quiet tones, periodically looking over our way as dad, David and I stood there together.

"Ah oh..." Dad said voicing his opinion. "Something tells me, this vacations about to get a bit more expensive."

"Why do you say that?" I asked.

"I've seen that look in your mother's eyes too many times before. Whenever I do...I know it's going to cost me something. And especially the way they're all sitting there huddled up together. They're up to something...that's for damn sure." There was laughter then, and hugs all around amongst the girls. They soon came wandering back towards us, though as mom looked at dad, she merely shook her head at him.

"I'll tell you later," she said simply.

We soon boarded the launch, once more heading back to our own huts. Moments after our arrival, I was comfortably asleep in my very own bed. My last thoughts as I drifted off...wondering what would no doubt happen next.

**

I was dreaming. And in my dream, I could feel the hot silkiness of my sister's cunt as it gathered me in. The feel of her free-flowing juices as they surrounded my prick. The subtle up and down movements, the softness of that textured sheath gripping my cock, squeezing it, holding it, kissing it with the most tenderness of embraces.

My eyes popped open just as my cock popped. I looked down, Stacy's mouth even then formed around my shaft, her cheeks billowing, puffing out as she endeavored to take and thus swallow what I knew had to be one hell of a big load.

"Thought I'd return the favor," she said, even as a bit of cum escaped the corner of her mouth though she was quick to capture it, licking it up again. Stacy gave my prick another half dozen or so cleansing sucks before suddenly sitting up.

"Where are you going?" I asked, half-groggy from dream-sleep, and unexpected enjoyable climax.

"We're going shopping. Mom's taking all the girls on a bit of a shopping trip over at the resort. Probably have lunch there, but back for the Luau of course. So prepare yourself," she laughed. "Maybe take advantage of the time and actually get a bit more sleep in. Something tells me...we're all going to need it."

"No wonder dad said what he did," I answered in response to that. "If mom's taking you all on a shopping spree...knowing you three, it IS apt to get expensive!"

"Knowing mom, and knowing what she has in mind, it very well could. Will just have to wait and see. But...I'm already looking forward to this evening Brad," she said leaning over to kiss me before scampering out the door. Once more, I could taste the essence of my own climax still clinging to her lips as she disappeared. I smiled, sighing pleasurably, and soon after drifted back off to sleep again.

**

I woke up a couple of hours later, hungry and thirsty. Wandering over to the main bungalow, I grabbed something to eat, washing that down with a cup of cold coffee, which wasn't half bad actually. Hearing voices just outside, I stepped out onto the small private little patio and beach area of my parents hut. As expected, dad and David were sitting there talking. What wasn't expected, was what they were doing at the time when I came out.

"Morning son. We were just getting started here if you'd care to join us."

I know I stood there looking on, words failing me for a moment. Each of them sitting there stroking their respective cocks, doing so with what appeared to be a pair of the girl's panties. Amusing to some extent was the sheepish expression on my brother's face as he sat there looking at me.

"These are Chris's," he said stopping briefly as he held them up showing them to me. "She gave them to me to use...just before they left. Thought I'd give it a try...see what I was missing out on," he added to that. Dad nodded towards another chair, glancing at it...seeing what appeared to be a silky-black pair of women's panties.

"Your moms. She left them for you," he said smiling. "Told me to tell you...she's expecting you to enjoy yourself for her."

I had to laugh. For a moment, the idea of the three of us just sitting around jerking ourselves off together with the girl's panties seemed almost absurd. Almost. But the reality was...standing there as dad continued on, though I wasn't sure whose panties he was currently using while he did, and as David then continued...the memories of doing so myself in the past came rushing back to me. As my cock began to quite naturally stiffen at the thought, I resigned myself into joining my father and brother in this somewhat kinky little indulgence. Dad smiled as I took my seat without saying anything further. I picked mom's panties up, holding them to my nose for a moment, smelling her musky fragrance as I did that.

"She slept in them last night, told me to tell you that."

I enjoyed their feel. Slinky, slick, especially the way they caressed my cock as I wrapped them around my swollen member and moved them up and down my shaft several times. David was grinning now too, obviously a bit more comfortable now that I had actually joined them. He seemed to be experimenting with Chris's panties, looping them around the bulbous head of his prick, and then twisting them back and forth. Even from where I was sitting, I could see a dollop of pre-cum fuck juice oozing from the head of my brother's dick.

"Amazing how good that really does feel," he spoke in a lusty tone of voice. "Just surprised I never thought about doing this until now."

"Ditto that," dad said. "Though thanks to Brad Junior here for letting mom catch him. If he hadn't, I might never have tried this myself either."

"I didn't let mom catch me," I said in my defense. "She just did. I honestly didn't think she'd come home as soon as she did...when she did."

"Whatever," dad mused. "Just glad she did, and then told me about it after that. I've been amusing myself once in a while this way ever since!"

Dad then turned to David. "Anyone ever catch you doing anything?" Dad asked curiously, slow stroking his cock, simply enjoying the pure pleasure of doing so, though heightening the arousal in his own speech as he did that.

Once again David looked a bit sheepish, but he too was really starting to get into this.

And perhaps the "sharing" of such stories was becoming an added turn on for him as well. "Well...you already know about most of that sort of thing," he began. "But you probably don't know about our next door neighbor, Mrs. Green."

"The old lady next door?" Dad interjected, suddenly interested, sitting up a bit though I noticed his hand slid down his partially exposed shaft several times in rapid succession. "No...I never heard anything, what happened?"

David laughed hearing and seeing dad's response to that as well. "Yeah, I used to think of her as 'Old Lady Green,' myself...until I saw something I wasn't supposed to one day. After that, I saw her in an entirely different light. I quietly had to laugh thinking back now myself. Mrs. Green had lived next door to us before we had moved into the larger house, which meant, dad was pretty close to her age now, though I didn't remind him of that as David continued.

"Yeah, I was weeding the garden that morning, the south strip next to the fence where our yard bordered hers. If you remember, it was my punishment for the fight I'd recently been in with Brad."

I remembered that too. I'd been assigned to do the Western strip next to the fence behind the house.

"I just happened to look up for a moment, just in time to see Mrs. Green cross in front of her bedroom window. She stood there looking out briefly, but hadn't seen me. I know...because I ducked down after spotting her. She didn't have a single stitch on! But what surprised me, was the fact she looked pretty damn good for her age. I had expected to see something else maybe. But what I saw was this fairly attractive looking woman, especially when I then saw her hand come down actually cupping one of her fairly large breasts. Sure...they weren't all firm and perky or anything, not even the way mom's look now. But like I said, they weren't half bad for a woman in her late sixties, trust me. Needless to say, I was stunned when she lifted it up, actually licking her own nipple! She soon stepped away from the window however, but that only left me curious as to what else she might be doing. That's when I jumped over the small fence and raced over to the backside of her house where her bedroom was."

"What happened then?" Dad asked, obviously even more excited now, his hand stroking his hard prick a bit more forcefully at this point, though then again...we all seemed to be, including David as he continued relating the story to us.

"Well of course I wasn't sure where she was at, or what she was doing at the moment. But the window was just low enough that I could peek in if I stood up on tiptoe. Trying to be as careful as possible, I looked in. Sure enough...she was still in the room, standing in front of her vanity, looking at herself. But it was what she was doing as she did that, that caught my attention. She was using a hairbrush on herself to masturbate with."

I remembered Chris telling me once she used to masturbate with her hairbrush too. I began to wonder if that wasn't the preferred method of choice until fancy vibrators finally made an appearance. Especially with the way some of the handles were shaped back then. I couldn't help wondering if the manufacturers actually knew what else they were being used for, and had purposely designed them that way.

"Admittedly, it was pretty fucking hot seeing this reasonably attractive woman standing they're playing with herself like that. So I began playing with myself while watching her, taking my cock out," he said looking down at himself now, a large wet spot clearly showing through the lighter color of the material as he held it over the tip of his cock, still rubbing himself with it. "I remember looking away just for a moment, sort of checking to make sure no one could see where I was from the house, and then looking back. Except when I did...there she was. Standing in the window right in front of me, looking down at me. Me...standing there with my cock in hand! I actually fell down, so startled upon seeing her, afraid of course that she was suddenly going to make a scene or something. You know...come running out, or worse...come over to the house and tell mom what she'd caught me doing. Only that didn't happen. Instead, she continued to stand there, which is when I noticed, she was still fucking herself with that damn hairbrush. And...she was smiling at me in a most sultry, horny way. Well fuck. I just sat there on the ground below, looking up at her, and proceeded to continue myself. Me jerking myself off watching her, and her doing the same...watching me."

"Damn son," dad laughed. "Who'd have thought Old Lady Green was such a horny old woman! But then I guess since she'd been widowed for a couple of years, that it stands to reason. Sort of makes me wish I'd have known that myself!"

"Mom would have skinned you alive," I told him. "Back then anyway."

"Possibly," dad snickered. "Though I doubt it. It was about that time that your mother and I started to experiment with things just a little. So it's entirely possible, we could have at the very least ended up in a threesome with her perhaps, though admittedly, I'm not sure Mrs. Green would have been accepting of that."

"Yeah, I don't think she would have been," David explained. "I know...because after that episode, we actually spoke about it once. About what happened. And that's when she told me that she had enjoyed what we had done, and that we could in fact do it again from time to time too. But only watching one another. Never touching. So we never did. But I spent many an hour watching Mrs. Green with that damn hairbrush of hers, and she spent many an hour watching me jerking myself off. Man that woman had a mouth on her when she got horny. She's have made a sailor blush let me tell you!"

"Fuck, I need to cum," dad suddenly announced. "Just thinking about the two of you doing that has got me almost there already."

"Yeah...me too," David said, obviously the thoughts of those past moments still filling his head. As for me, I was myself lost in the memory of that day when mom walked in on me there in her bathroom. The way I had turned suddenly, only then realizing she was there, just as my cock began to unleash the torrent of cream that it did, drenching and covering my mother's blouse almost to the point of transparency.

The sound of dad's grunt announced the arrival of his climax. David and I both looking over towards him, though more specifically at his cock. The green satin panties he was using appeared to be those I had seen Jessica wearing before. In seconds however, I watched the material darken considerably, and even some of his discharge appear to actually seep through the thin material as he finished jacking himself off.

"Oh fuck!" David cried out seconds later. He leaned forward in his chair just a little, the light blue panties he still had wrapped around his cock, one hand holding onto one end, the other pulling on the opposite end as he simply tugged them back and forth, working his cock off that way. Head exposed, I watched it explode, several streamers of his thick sticky semen suddenly bursting from the tip, arching out a bit as though suspended for a moment before simply falling downwards into the sand. It was an impressive display, soon triggering my own orgasmic release. Though like dad, I too covered my prick tip, enjoying the sexy feel of mom's sheer black panties. Just sheer enough however, that even as my seed erupted, most of that still came through the material of her panties soaking my hand. The stark contrast however obscenely decadent in another way. The milky white substance coating and covering the black material, oozing out in thick white globs that pooled on the surface, even as I folded them over, trying to capture the rest of it as I came.

The three of us sat back, quietly enjoying the moment. I couldn't help sitting there shaking my head a few minutes later. I was twenty one years old, and had just had my first ever circle jerk, with my father and brother no less.

**

It was late in the afternoon before the girls returned from their excursion over on the main island. I was surprised that they hadn't come back with more than they did, not much than a few small trinkets perhaps. Mom gave me an inquiring look almost the moment they got back. I smiled, nodding my head at her, to which she brightened considerably, smiling back, and almost immediately headed inside to their bungalow. No doubt to see if I had indeed placed her panties back onto her bed. Which I had done.

Stacy too came up to me, an even bigger smile on her face as she gave me a kiss on the cheek. "Feel like going for a swim with me up at the pool?" She asked.

"Sure, I was just thinking about that in fact," I told her, though it soon became obvious that David, Jessica as well as Chris wanted to come along too. I was hoping for some private time, perhaps getting down to the bottom of what was really going on here...but that was obviously going to have to wait as the five of us then left, hiking up to the falls together.

We played and frolicked together in the slightly cooler water there beneath the falls for the better part of an hour. Eventually making the short climb up to the plateau again, where we spread out our towels, laying down, and letting the warmth from the sun overhead dry us off.

Chris, Jessica and David soon seemed to be dozing off. Stacy and I however laying side by side simply looking and smiling at one another.

"So...what did you guys get?" I asked curiously. "As worried as dad was initially, it didn't appear to me like you bought the farm when you guys came back."

Stacy smiled. "Not so much buying stuff, mom just needed to check on the arrangements for the Luau tonight more than anything else, and then a couple of other minor surprises, is all."

"Ah uh," I said not fully accepting her explanation. I knew the Luau had been planned and already paid for, and couldn't imagine there could be much more that mom had needed to add to that, or see to regarding it. So whatever else was going on...I was obviously out of the loop, and my tight-lipped sister wasn't saying anything more to me about it either.

"Just be patient," she said then. "You'll see," she smiled, and then reached down wrapping her tiny little hand around my very soft, very flaccid...very small cock. Even in her hand, it disappeared. "Wake it up," she said waggling it a bit. "I want to see it squirt."

"I don't know how much it would, not yet anyway," I informed her. "We sort of did that already just a short time before you guys got back."

"Yeah I know," she giggled. "Figured you might. We were talking about that during lunch, Chris mentioning the fact that everyone had given you guys a pair of their panties to jerk off into. Obviously...you must have gotten moms. I can only imagine what she's doing with them now," Stacy laughed seductively.

"And with dad no doubt watching her too," I added to that.

"No doubt. Anyway, I really am looking forward to the Luau tonight, should be fun. Mom did make a couple of small changes to that, in order to spice things up some. Wait until you see," she grinned.

I was curious, but then again if it was indeed a surprise, I was willing to wait and see what transpired as the evening wore on. Stacy continued to waggle my dick however, which finally had started to stiffen some.

"On second thought...maybe we should wait," she seemed to decide, though giving it one last tug, as it was hard now, it slapped back against my chest as she let go of it, actually standing before I could even say anything. "I'm heading back...time for a nice little nap myself, especially if the evening is going to be a long one, which I'm inclined to think it very well will be." I stood then myself, joining her for the walk back.

"Tease," I spat looking at her sexy little ass as I followed her down the trail, my now rock hard cock following her.

She looked back over her shoulder at me, giggling. "You ain't seen nothing yet big brother," and then like a shot, she took off back to the huts in a dead run, leaving me to stand there watching her sweet sexy body disappear through the palm trees shortly after that.

I was half tempted to stand there and jerk one off though, and might have had I not heard the others soon coming up behind me. Chris appeared taking my arm in hers, hugging me close to her as we walked along. She smiled at me knowingly. Once more telling me that the girls were sharing way too many secrets amongst one another. I opened my mouth to speak, but she just winked, making a motion across her lips as though zipping them, which essentially spoke volumes to me.

The evening now, couldn't come soon enough.

**

We had of course all more appropriately dressed for the trip back over to the resort. Though even then the girls wore floral print bikini tops, with matching sarongs. I wore my favorite Hawaiian shirt, which was an exact replica of the one worn throughout most of the Magnum P.I. series by Tom Selleck, along with a pair of white shorts. Dad and David both were similarly attired as we made our way over to the island in preparation for our own private little Luau.

After we arrived, we were then escorted down to an area of the beach that had been cordoned off. Several privacy screens had also been set up, thus blocking anyone's view of the beach area we'd be dining at, ensuring that for whatever reason, we would indeed have plenty of privacy from prying eyes up closer to the resort.

The table was already spread with several delicacies, two men just then uncovering the roasted pig that had been cooking in the ground since early morning, or even late last night. Tiki torches burning in several places as the major source of light, though it also appeared there would be a nice sized bonfire that would also be lit later on that evening. The biggest surprise came when I noticed that four more place settings had been prepared around the ground level table we'd be sitting at. And sure enough, just as we arrived, I glanced up just in time to see that Bill, Barbra, John and Jill would be joining us.

"Made arrangements to invite our new friends," mom announced. "After all, we have plenty of food, more than enough...and thought it might be fun having them join us for this evening."

It was nice to see them again, and I was beginning to imagine the way the night might go now after seeing them, curious if that would happen here...or elsewhere. Though the large privacy screens which had been set up hinted at the latter rather than the former. We soon enjoyed a few cocktails as last minute preparations for the meal was complete, and then proceeded to eat, dining on a myriad of fine food and delicacies. Midway through the meal, the evening entertainment showed up. Several very beautiful and attractive Polynesian women who'd be performing several Native dances for us. The thing was, for this dance at least, and several others hopefully...they wouldn't be wearing coconuts as bras. Every single one of them was bare breasted as they began the first of what I could only describe as sultry, if not downright sexual fertility dances for our entertainment.

Before long, even the bonfire was lit. Male dancers now joining the women, scantily dressed themselves, their almost bare asses giving the girls something exciting to watch, while the guys continued ogling all the bare breasted women. They had even returned for the bonfire dance, wearing what could only be described as "mini" grass skirts. Their own asses periodically showing, and hinted evidence of the fact, they were wearing nothing more on beneath those either!

These dances now taking place around the bonfire of course, a bit further away from where we were sitting, using a lot more light and shadow as the performers began. And then as they began, the men and women dancing close, even intimately together, it appeared at times, without coming right out and revealing it, there was a lot more going on here than what met the eye.

"Are they really fucking?" Bill asked looking on, though I think that question was on my lips as well. It certainly looked like a few were, though as they slowly emerged from around one side of the bonfire where they were more easily seen, if they had been...they had separated just at that point, though joining together once again just as they began to disappear around the backside of the fire where the light possibly was playing tricks on us. I honestly couldn't be sure. But either way...it was erotic as hell.

Eventually all the girls were coaxed into performing a dance with the professional dancers. And much to everyone's delight, they all took of their bikini tops too, now dancing topless as well, adding additional delight to the provocative performance. An obvious "shimmy" being required in some places, and then a slow moving, almost hypnotic series of undulations in another. Even Chris made light of herself, along with Barbra and Jill as they all three tried desperately to make their tit's wobble and bounce the way the others were in various places. All to no avail of course, it just wasn't physically possible. But it was still funny.

As the night began to wear down, I was starting to wonder. As entertaining as this all had been, there had to be more to it than just this. Even when Jill, Barbra, John and Bill said their goodnights, thanking mom and dad for letting the four of them join us, I was wondering then if things hadn't been sort of put on hold...waiting for the four of them to actually leave. Though if indeed that was the case, why had they been invited then in the first place? I was still puzzling that one out when we began making our way back to the launch. Still early yet, not even close to ten o'clock at this point, I realized that whatever else was going to happen, would happen...back on our own private little island. And it didn't take long for that to be confirmed either. Though I, along with both Dad and David where taken by surprise when it was.

"Ok boys...you three have to wait here for a minute," mom told us. "So don't go running off anywhere. And you'll know where to go when the times right. So just behave, stay where you are...and wait for the signal."

"What signal?" Dad asked.

"You'll know it when you see it," mom said turning around and leaving us at this point, though the other girls had already done so.

"I knew there was more to all this than what she was telling me," dad said, though smiling as he did so. "Though whatever it is...I have a feeling, it'll be well worth it."

We continued to stand for several precious minutes, getting more and more fidgety and anxious until suddenly the tropical forest just beyond, suddenly seemed to light up like a Christmas tree.

"What the hell?" David questioned speaking for all of us. It was as though someone had turned landing lights on...one by one, a series of Tiki torches suddenly lit, running up the trail away from the bungalows, and well beyond, running back up to where the falls were.

"I think...that's the signal," dad said easily enough. "Come on...let's go see what this is all about," as he then led on without waiting any further. David and I quickly following, now more than curious ourselves. Beyond, and just ahead of us, more and more torches were lit, easily showing the way in the almost total darkness, yet there was no sign of anyone, nor could we see anyone actually lighting them, though the distance was still great enough to keep us from seeing that. The effect however, was quite spectacular in its simplicity. As we finally drew close enough to the actual location of the falls, here too was a scene that seemed almost surreal in design. Several torches had been placed, encircling the pond beyond. The waterfall now shimmering and sparkling in the light, looking at times like glass, at other times like a strobe light going off, as it fooled the eyes.

"Where the hells the girls?" I stood wondering, as none of us yet had even seen anyone.

"They must be..."

Suddenly the top of the plateau was lit up, two additional bonfires immediately erupting almost magically.

"Up there..." David finished as we all stood looking upwards now. As the light from the bonfires intensified and brightened, an entirely unexpected, different image suddenly appeared.

"Holy...fucking shit! Are you seeing what I'm seeing?" I asked. But as neither David nor Dad spoke, looking where I was...it was quite evident they were too. And they were just as speechless as I suddenly was. I only then glanced around, honestly, and seriously expecting to see some gigantic hairy creature come bounding in, descending down upon us. Looking back and up again...seeing my sweet, bare-assed naked sister as she hung on some sort of a platform, her hands bound, tied above her head. For the moment at least, looking limp, totally subdued. I again asked myself..."Just what the fuck is going on here? And why is Stacy all bound and tied up like that?"

We were about to find out.

CHAPTER 4

Once again dad took off at a run, following the path leading around the side of the hill up towards the plateau. I ran directly behind him, with David behind me. As we turned the corner beginning the slight ascent, another torch greeted us just above. This one being held however, by Chris who stood there looking down at us as we approached. She was wearing a bright white bikini, highlighting her dark tan. Any other time I'd have looked on admiring the look. At the moment however, with my sister dangling naked on a well designed platform, seeing Chris was the furthest thing on my mind.

"What the hell's going on anyway?" Dad asked as he got within distance from my sister. Reaching her, she put out her hand, pressing it against dad's chest, effectively stopping him. At least she was smiling.

"You'll see soon enough," she explained, though stepping in front of him once more as he made a small attempt to pass by her. "Wait here. I promise...you won't be disappointed." Confused, dad remained where he was, even as Chris reached behind herself, suddenly producing what appeared to be an ornamental knife of some sort, handing it to me by the blade.

"Jesus," David spoke just behind me, but said nothing else, no doubt as confused as dad and I were by this rather strange behavior we were all seeing.

"Go rescue your sister," Chris told me as I took the knife from her, only then stepping to the side, allowing me...and only me to pass by her. I looked back, but she had again blocked the way, dad and David both standing there looking on with questions on their faces. A short walk further, and I was soon standing on the summit of the plateau, only now...just ahead, flanked by two more burning torches that had been planted on either side of the path, I saw my mother and Jessica, similarly dressed as Chris had been. Each wearing white, very revealing bikini's, only they both held something else in their hands as well. As I drew near, I realized then that they appeared to be spears as they stopped me, crossing them. I glanced ahead, off a short distance, the platform that Stacy was still hanging from.

"Are those for real?" I asked glancing back at the two of them. They certainly looked real anyway.

"Want to find out?" Jessica joked, though I was finding this crazy scene a bit much at the moment. Mom tossed Jessica a withering look however, and then formally addressed me.

"Remove your clothing first, and then you may pass," she said looking fairly serious now. Whatever was going on here, though I was confident it was all some sort of silly game, I did as she'd asked. Removing the shorts and shirt I had on, I was soon naked. Only then did they uncross the spears blocking my way, turning as though invitation to continue on, which I did.

Though the path led directly towards where Stacy was, I noticed something else now just off and behind the platform itself. It looked totally out of place, unsure of what it even was until I drew closer, only then seeing it for what it actually was.

"Holy shit!" I actually chuckled, now realizing. The lengths that mom had actually gone with all this suddenly dawning on me...not to mention the cost that poor dad would soon be hearing about no doubt. What I now saw was a very crude, yet elaborately made bed. White sheets adorning it, standing a good three feet off the ground. Thick rounded beams and poles all woven together with grass-roped cords. A sacrificial alter in a way perhaps, now giving me a much truer sense of what this was all about. I shook my head in disbelief, and yet excitement too, only now realizing what it was that was actually being offered here. I turned once more, looking back, now seeing that Chris, dad and David had reached mom and Jessica, though the two of them continued to stand guard, holding everyone at bay there behind me. I continued on, the knife held in my hand, following the path towards the edge of the cliff, which overlooked the pool and falls beyond. The platform jutting out just a little, not so much as to truly look all that dangerous as well made as it was. But the illusion of what had been created, and seen from below, had been brilliant in its design. Hearing my approach at this point, Stacy finally rolled her head, looking over towards me. I could see the nervous smile on her face.

I stood in front of her, just admiring her for a moment, now knowing my part in this carefully designed play. "I'm here to rescue, seduce you...I think," I told her holding the knife, knowing what it was I was supposed to now do. "This is really what you want? Me to be the one?" I asked needing to be sure.

"It is yes..." she responded back. "But not to be seduced...to be taken, savagely," she added to that. "I want you...to fuck me!"

I knew then that Stacy wanted...needed this, to be an experience she'd always remember. Something very special, which it would be...for both of us. But perhaps not in quite the same way that mom had initially intended. It was time to improvise just a little.

I looked back, once more seeing our entire family slowly approaching us now. Each one carrying a torch, though mom and Jessica still wielded their wicked looking spears too. I briefly hoped that Jessica wouldn't get too far involved in her own role in this, and actually use hers on me when they realized what I was actually about to do here.

I raised the knife, though not in the stance of slicing through the bindings that held my sister's wrists or legs together, securing her to the beam jutting out over her head. Instead, I brought it up, almost in a stabbing motion, coming down with it, impaling the blade in a cross-support beam nearby. Even Stacy looked at me questioningly upon seeing that.

"I think you'll enjoy this even better than the bed," I informed her. "Especially for your first time...far more memorable," I finished, though adding as I spoke silently to myself..."I hope."

I could sense the rest of the family suddenly stopping a short distance away, no doubt wondering...curious as they stood looking on. I knew Stacy certainly was as she glanced towards me, as I stepped closer towards her. Spread-eagle as she was, her legs though comfortably bound, giving me the perfect opportunity here as I closed the last bit of distance between us. I cupped her breasts in my hands, molding them together even more than they were. I leaned forward, pressing the stiffness of my hard cock against her flesh, nowhere's near her pussy yet, but letting her feel, and perhaps wonder at my intent. Gathering her breasts, I kissed and sucked them as one. Her hard aroused extended nipples pressed together as I drew them simultaneously into my mouth, sucking them, molding and caressing her breasts as I did. My cock spearing her upper abdomen as I stood there paying homage to her breasts.

"Oh god!" She moaned loudly. "Yes...yes! Fuck yes!" She cried out, loud enough I am sure everyone heard her, and in doing so....stopping them once more a short distance away from us as they now encircled, looking on. No doubt surprised by this slight change of plans, they appeared pleased however as I took my time here, savoring the delights of my still bound sister before finally rescuing her and releasing her bonds.

"You wanted savage...I'm about to give you savage," I said leaning closer, now whispering in her ear so that only she could hear me when I said that.

I heard her sigh, moaning deeply, excitedly. "Oh Brad," she said simply.

I placed the head of my blood engorged cock between her legs. Felt the liquid essence of her very aroused cunt already bathing the tip of my prick as I teased her with it a little.

"Fuck me...oh god yes, fuck me...right here, right now," she suddenly cried out, her words reverberating out over the water below, and through the small canyon like area that was formed there. I knew how easily everyone else had heard her too, and half wondered just how far her cry of desire and arousal might have actually carried on our own little island.

If there had indeed been a furry King Kong anywhere's close to us, he'd no doubt have heard, and even then been reaching us...his massive fists already reaching out to tear her away from me. But it would have been too late for that even then. I shoved, my prick impaling my sister's cunt...spearing her deeply in one sudden thrust. She cried out again, ungodly sounds slicing through the peaceful silence of the night. I thrust once more, even harder this time, deeper as she cried out again, thrashing wildly there in front of me, straining against the binds that still held her. I pinched and pulled on her nipples almost cruelly, still thrusting hard, deep and fast into my swinging, swaying sister. But all that did, was seemingly intensify her delight, her ear-piercing scream, once more echoing off the rocks and falls, reverberating all around us like a thunder clap as she continued to cry out over, and over, and over again.

Still thrusting, still fucking, I glanced up briefly, only now spotting the others, all pretense of game, theatre, or act suddenly evaporating in an instant. Mother was already down on her knees before David. His hands on the back of her head, fucking my mother's face, almost idiotically holding onto the spear for support which he had impaled into the ground next to her. Jessica and Chris too, dragging dad down to the hard ground beneath them. Chris already grinding herself on dad's cock, Jessica doing the same to his face, though heads turned towards Stacy and I still looking on.

Though they couldn't possibly hear it, I could...not to mention feeling it as I pummeled my sister's cunt almost unmercifully. Hearing the almost frothy like juices, even feeling them as they ran out of her cunt, bathing my shaft and balls, literally dripping and then running down her legs. We stood, churning fuck-butter together, the hard-felt slap of flesh stinging flesh, her cries of ecstasy, followed by my own now. Though ours weren't the only sounds of the night, the wild unleashed frenzy taking place only a short distance away, animalistic in nature. Mom now on all fours, David behind, rutting with her there. Dad too, having switched positions with my sisters, fucking Chris from behind, as she in turn now ate Jessica in a mutual "69". Dad no doubt reaping the benefits of that, as Jessica licked, sucked and pleased the two of them together.

But there were other sounds as well. As though the entire forest had seemingly come alive, waking up to the erotic frenzy now taking place. I tried to gather my wits about me, making sense out of it, but too far gone for that at the moment to really care. The slickness of my sister's cunt, the first pulsating contractions as she hovered on the edge of climatic bliss, soon stole all thought, care and concern. I felt my own orgasm rapidly approaching now, my breath coming in pants of unearthly lust and desire.

"Come in me...come with me!" Stacy screamed out one last time, feeling that first massive spurt as it exploded from my cock, filling her. She met it with an equal force of her own, the sudden unexpected, unanticipated deluge of her own spurting. I felt the force of it as it literally sprayed out, nearly dislodging me. The rapture of her liquid climax bathing the two of us, soaking the ground, the platform, and everything else as well. My own discharge meeting hers, joining it, and then backwashed as she continued to spurt long, almost continuous streamers of girl spunk into the night.

All about us came the cries of similar ecstasy's taking place. Almost as though the entire universe had somehow gotten involved. Drained, almost too weak to stand, I half collapsed, only then grabbing the knife up again, this time slicing easily and quickly through the bonds holding my sister's feet. And then upwards, I took the knife parting the rope that had secured her hands. They quickly parted from the beam as she literally fell into my arms. Once more I thrust the knife into the wood leaving it, turning, only a few feet precariously from the ledge, holding onto her, peering over...looking below.

"Holy fucking shit...would you look at that," I said. But Stacy was as yet too far gone to even entertain any thoughts of doing that, barely clinging to me as I stood there holding my almost unconscious sister.

I'd have made bets that half the island was now sitting below us likewise engaged in what could only be described as an orgy of unprecedented decadence. It was the most amazing sight I had ever seen. And one I certainly hadn't expected to see as I stood there looking down.

**

I had no idea how they had all gotten here...or when. But gathered all about below us, like a writhing snake upon the sands, stood a throng of people, at least a hundred strong or so it seemed. A massive orgy of flesh at this point, everyone joined or coupled about, save for just a few, still looking up watching. I noticed then, looking further, raising my own hand in recognition, waving...as Bob, John, Barbra and Jill looked on, waving back. And then as though the water itself and risen, casting a gigantic wave over the top of them, they fell back into the sea of flesh surrounding them, and were quickly consumed.

I carried Stacy off the platform, now walking back towards the bed, even as the rest of the family gathered themselves, once more holding onto their torches, following us.

"No point in wasting all this," I told Stacy as she finally smiled looking up at me. "Especially after all the time and effort mom went to in setting all this up." I gently placed her down onto the bed now, climbing in after her as the family stood, gathered around. I was surprised when David leaned over the bed, kissing Stacy on the forehead.

"I'd be lying if I said I wasn't a little jealous of Brad," he told her. "But that...was the most amazing thing I had ever seen, and you couldn't have picked anyone more perfect for finally doing it," he said, likewise holding his hand out towards me. I took it, but then pulled him closer, actually gathering him into an embrace.

"About damn fucking time," mom said just under her breath, though we all snickered quietly together at her comment.

"Listen, we've already done what was come here to do," Stacy offered. "And this bed is certainly big enough...for all of us," she now added to that. "So come on mom...dad," she said smiling at the two of them, "It's about time I found out the rest of what I've been missing."

"Sloppy thirds?" I laughed looking at David, though he just shrugged his shoulders grinning from ear to ear.

"Works for me bro..." he grinned once more. "I'm starting to get used to it," he added to that. And then crawled into the bed next to Stacy, watching as dad slowly eased his hard stiff cock into the depths of my little sister's cunt.

"Well hell...while we're waiting here," mom said climbing onto the bed at that moment, already easing herself down over my brother's cock, she then turned looking back over her shoulder towards me. "Don't just stand there," she said. "Slick that bad boy up...I've got another place you can put that you know. Always wondered what it might feel like having the two of you inside me...at the same time that is," she laughed adding to that. "Not like the first time...that's for damn sure."

I was doing just that, though Chris offered up a bit of her own spit, grinning wickedly before turning, hand in hand with Jessica as the two of them began walking off.

"Where you two going?" I asked.

"Crowded enough on the bed as it is," she told me. "Thought we'd go down and mingle below...when you're finished here, you'll know where to 'come' and find us," she said winking, emphasizing the play on words. She and Jessica then headed off, running and laughing wildly as they headed down to the orgy still taking place below us.

"Oh baby...you are so juicy wet honey!" Dad said as he began moving in and out of Stacy's now devirginized womanhood.

"Well, Brad certainly had a lot to do with that daddy," she told him. "I think I'll be leaking his cum juice out of me for days after this. And yours too hopefully," she added to that. "And yours too David," she then said turning to him as well. "Provided of course, you still have some left for me after fucking mommy," she giggled.

"No worries baby...I have an idea as to how to redeposit it for you if you'd like...after he has," she told her.

"Ok, even I have to admit, I'd enjoy seeing you do that," I responded in kind as now prepared, I eased my own hard stiff shaft into the tight little opening of my mother's ass, where David sat patiently, waiting for me to join him there.

It was an amazingly odd sensation. Feeling my brothers cock pressing against my own, only the thinnest of obstacles actually separating the two of us as we began moving in and out of my mother's twin holes respectively.

Watching, Stacy reached out, giving one of mom's swaying breasts a gentle tweak. "And thank you mommy...for doing all this," she told her as David and I continued, sawing away at mom's body like a couple of lumberjacks cutting down trees.

"Hey...what about me?" Dad questioned, though he too was still enjoying himself, busily thrusting away inside my sister's extremely slippery pussy, which we could now all hear quite easily again. "I'm the one actually paying for all this," he said reminding himself that he still had no real idea how much all of this actually had cost. Or how...mom had even managed to do all this in such a relatively short period of time...all things considered.

"I think I'm in the process of thanking you right now," she responded back to that. "Don't you think?" She asked winking at him, to which he winked back. "Yes...yes you are honey. And whatever this does end up costing me, will be well worth it too."

"Won't be nearly as bad as you think honey," mom responded back to dad with a deep groan as David and I seemed to get into a near perfect rhythm here...one in, and one out as it were, fucking mom's holes, pleasuring her beyond the limit.

"I've already paid for a portion of this...in other ways," she giggled slightly. "Not to mention the fact, most of the workers and staff that were involved in putting all this together, are no doubt down there, enjoying themselves," she said looking towards the falls, even though none of us could really see anything. Though the sounds of laughter, ongoing moans and groans seemed to be drifting up towards us almost non-stop anyway.

Once more Stacy began panting like crazy, wrapping her legs around my father's back as he began spearing her even more forcefully. She was obviously closing in on yet again another mind-blowing orgasm. Just as David and I were. With a nod of our heads towards one another, we immediately picked up the pace just a little, mom's eyes suddenly opening wide as we did that.

"Oh my god!" She cried out. And then seconds later, bathed us in her own little deluge.

**

Once again spent, David and I both, along with Dad, sat lounging on the bed simply watching now, still collecting our breaths. As promised, mom had climbed over towards Stacy, me helping to support her on one side, as Stacy lay partially on her back, though lifting her ass, pussy to pussy with mother as she sat astride her, scissoring her in a way.

"That's it...just hold still, let me do all the work," she then added to that, grinding a bit even then however. "Can you feel that?" she soon asked.

"I can! Oh my god...I can! All that cum..."

"From me to you baby...just like I said," mom said grinding harder now, squishing about... two sloppy went cunts kissing one another. Not too unexpectedly either, they soon came again, while doing that.

"Well as much as I hate to admit it, I am plumb tuckered out," I stated. And though the orgy was no doubt still going on, there wasn't more than a couple of hours before sunrise. "I'm heading off to bed," I informed everyone, though pleasantly surprised when Stacy soon joined me, taking my hand.

"Me too," she stated giving everyone a kiss goodnight, and then falling in behind me as we made our way back down the trail again, passing by the now much calmer sea of nudity all laying about, though some still moving, still somehow engaged, not quite ready to give it all up yet.

"Wonder where the other girls are," Stacy questioned as we quietly stepped by.

"Almost afraid to ask," I said actually stepping over one woman, who I only then recognized as one of the Polynesian dancers we'd seen performing at the Luau earlier that evening...or rather the night before as I now thought about it.

We made it back to my bungalow, stepping inside, both surprised to see Chris laying there in my bed waiting for us.

"About damn time," she grinned. "I've been waiting for you."

Stacy and I looked at one another and laughed.

"Oh hell...no plans for today anyway," I told her. "We can sleep away the rest of the day if we want to."

"Maybe so," Stacy tossed. "But my poor little pussies a bit tender at the moment. Not used to doing that just yet, so I may have to take a rain check myself here anyway."

"Nonsense," Chris told her. "All it needs is a little tender loving care. So come here honey...let big sister take care of that for you."

As tired as I honestly was, I was more than happy to let the girls play doctor, as within minutes, I was sound asleep, peacefully drifting off to the sounds of my little sister's soft sweet joyful moaning.

**

I had never been much of a golfer, and as such, had no desire to take the launch back over to the resort the following day. And besides, I was still exhausted and a bit hung-over from the night before. Dad and David however were both avid golfers, and had been looking forward to playing eighteen holes on the championship course they had over there. They were both gone, and no doubt already teeing up by the time I awoke, surprised to some extent to find myself alone when I did. I had honestly expected to wake up sandwiched between Chris and Stacy, neither one of which was there as I stretched, yawned, and then reached down scratching myself. The sun was already well up as I stepped into the outside shower, rinsing off god knows what before heading off in search of everyone else.

I figured that by now, as late as it was already, I'd more than likely find them all gathered together at the main bungalow. Sure enough, they were, though I was somewhat relieved to see that most of them hadn't been up for much longer than I'd been. Though Stacy and Chris both looked like they had at least caught up on some sleep, looking a bit more relaxed and fresh, Jessica looked like something the cat had dragged in. Her hair was still fairly messy, having not even put a comb or a brush through it yet. And mom didn't look much better, though I didn't very often see her without makeup like she was now. Everyone quietly sipping coffee together as though the slightest sound would sound like a volcano erupting right about now.

"Coffee?" Stacy asked upon seeing me, almost in a whisper, still trying to hide a bit of a smile as she redirected my glance back towards mom. "Still trying to figure out if she's alive this morning," she added to that in an even lower, quieter tone of voice. Chris however wasn't quite as caring as Stacy had been, speaking up normally, though she received a hard glare from both Jessica and mom when she did that.

"Didn't feel like hitting any balls this morning huh?" Chris asked handing me a freshly brewed cup of coffee.

"Not my thing. Stroking them maybe...hitting them? No," I answered simultaneously thanking her for the coffee. I turned towards Stacy who was sitting next to me. "And how're you doing sis? How's your pussy feel?"

Any other time, such a question wouldn't have even been asked, before now anyway. And yet now, it seemed the most natural question in the world to be asking her under the circumstances.

"A bit tender perhaps," she giggled quietly. "But certainly ready, willing and able to go again," she soon added to that, even bringing a smile to mom's face upon hearing her say that.

"As tired as I am...I've still got a bit of an itch myself too," she smiled, though groaning simultaneously, lowering her own voice in speaking again as though the sound of actually speaking annoyed herself. "Once this headache goes away anyway."

"You know the best thing for a headache, is a good old fashioned orgasm," Chris offered.

"Really? You're kidding right?"

"No really. I read that it is, and then tried it out for myself. Unfortunately, most people don't feel much like having an orgasm when they have a headache, so they don't even attempt to try. As for myself...that's one of the reasons that neither Stacy nor I have one this morning, unlike the two of you," she said looking over at Jessica, who was looking even more miserable now as she continued to sit there. "We gave each other a very nice one earlier this morning."

"And where was I during all this?" I asked curiously.

"Right beside the two of us...snoring away. We were actually hoping you might wake up and join us, but we let you sleep instead, though like I said...we certainly managed to have a good time without you."

I laughed. "So you woke up doing, what you were doing when you went to sleep."

"Something along those lines," Chris agreed. "I have to admit, if I didn't like cock so much, I'd be half tempted to totally go the other way, especially as good as Stacy is at eating pussy."

"Yeah?" Mom spoke up, eyes interested as she looked over at her. "You really were serious about the orgasm thing yes?"

"Oh yeah, like I said...best thing ever for it, certainly works for me anyway."

"How about it Stacy? Feel like helping your mother out here?" She asked.

Stacy grinned. "Sure thing mom, how about you lay back that lounge chair there, and let me see what I can do for you."

Mom did that, undoing the robe she actually had on, confirming the fact she was still naked beneath it. Propping her head up just a little so she could still watch, Stacy knelt on another of the lounge cushions, positioning herself between mother's legs.

I sat still sipping my coffee, watching the two of them now, and found myself quickly becoming aroused again as I did so. Likewise wearing a soft fluffy robe, I hadn't tied mine however, so my cock was free to grow and expand as I sat there watching this. Chris and Jessica certainly noticed, Chris even reaching over at one point to give it a bit of a fondle herself. In the meantime, whatever magic Stacy was using on mom, appeared to be working. It wasn't long before mom was squeezing and playing with her own breasts, moaning and groaning quite audibly and pleasurably now.

"See? Told you...really does work wonders," Chris smiled approvingly as we continued watching the two of them.

"Ok, I'll bite...but I'd prefer a nice hard cock right now. Brad? You interested in helping me out?" Jessica asked.

Frankly I was surprised by her request. Throughout most of this, she and I had actually had very little contact. Even when things had opened up sexually amongst all of us, she and I had seemingly continued on with our mutual dislike of one another. So hearing her asking me to fuck her was an unexpected, unanticipated surprise.

"Sure...where and how would you like to?" I asked. She answered by simply standing up, dropping the robe she'd been wearing, now naked as well. Coming over, she merely straddled my lap as I sat there in my chair. I even had to place my coffee cup back onto the table lest I spill it on her. In seconds, I felt her somewhat dry, not yet lubricated pussy trying to force itself down over my not quite hard member. Though it wasn't long before she managed it, and that I was. I was soon deeply embedded in Jessica's cunt for the very first time. She was even smiling a little too as she looked down at the two of us, now fully joined.

"You feel every bit as good as David does inside me," she complimented. Yet again another surprise. "I guess you two are pretty close in size after all," she now added to that, finally starting to move a little, now sliding up and down my shaft as she got juicier and juicier. "Do that thing to my tits, that you were doing to Stacy's," she then asked. "I liked the way that looked...never did that," she added.

"You never had both of your tits sucked at the same time?" I asked incredulously, knowing her.

"Well...not by the same person," she grinned. "Not like that anyway."

Pressing her breasts together in order to suck both nipples simultaneously was even easier than it had been with Stacy. And though her breasts were only slightly larger, they weren't quite as firm or as full as Stacy's were either. A lot more malleable perhaps as I molded, pressing them against one another, her nipples easily coming together as I quickly placed my mouth over the two of them...sucking them together.

"Hmm, that IS nice," she moaned happily, now grinding more than sliding up and down, preferring to give a bit more stimulation to her clit perhaps as she found the perfect spot and position in doing so, grinding away at my shaft. I didn't mind it so much either, making it easier for me to continue sucking on her breasts, now nursing her twin nipples quite firmly, which she seemed to be very much enjoying at the moment.

"Damn..." Chris sighed almost mournfully watching me do that. "That's the ONE thing I'll NEVER get to experience myself," she complained again. "Not to mention the fact, that I'm suddenly sitting here...odd woman out. Again." I saw her reach over, suddenly grabbing a banana from off the table out of the fruit bowl. Pulling up her chair so that she could watch all of us, she then lifted her legs, placing them comfortably on the table, spreading herself. In seconds, she was easing the banana in and out of her cunt with a nice slow easy rhythm that she seemed to be thoroughly enjoying.

Hearing mom, I glanced over towards she and Stacy. She was just then gripping the sides of the lounge chair she was in, arching her back, lifting her ass. "Oh my god! Right there! Right there! Right there!" she literally cried out, forcing my sister to rise with her as she did that, hanging on, her mouth now glued to mom's cunt like a suction cup.

"God I know EXACTLY how that feels!" Chris cried out as well, now slamming that yellow banana unabashedly in and out of herself, the sounds of her female nectar easily heard as she seemed to be producing gallons of it. "Stacy's got a tongue on her like nobody's business!"

Even Jessica was looking over and watching this now, though she was once more moving up and down on my cock like a runaway freight train. "Oh fuck, oh fuck...yes, yes...come, come!" She called out, almost urging mom to do so, as though trying to gage and time her own climax to moms, just as I now guessed, that Chris was doing, as she too began urging mom to do the same.

"Come mother, come! That's it...come mother, let it go...let us see you come," she called out just as Jessica now was, though I could already feel my sister's pussy beginning to clench and pulsate about my shaft, so I knew that only moments more now, she would be.

It was precisely then, that mother came however, once more clenching at the chair, lifting herself even higher up than before. Suddenly the sounds of Stacy gurgling, trying to keep her mouth on mom's gushing cunt even then, though failing a moment later. Reluctantly sitting back, though pleased at her obvious handiwork as mom's pussy continued to spurt what looked to be like little pulsating fountains of pussy juice, one right after the other. I sat watching this, fascinated, as she sprayed all over my sister's breasts now. Stacy even went so far as to cup one of her own breasts, leaning forward, and now rubbing and smearing this against the still gushing opening of my mother's cunt, as though trying to put a plug in the dike...so to speak.

Chris was coming now too though, as was Jessica, and then I. Like dominoes falling, one orgasm after the other being triggered by everyone else's. I felt my own release as I began spurting massive volumes of cum inside my sister's cunt. The liquefied sounds of her release, now joining mine as the squishy, frothy mixture of girl cum and boy cum mingled together, soon after running out of her in torrents, drenching my balls in rivers of creamy thick pussy foam.

And just as we'd all climaxed simultaneously, we soon collapsed, pleasantly exhausted, breaths still labored as we sat trying to collect ourselves.

"Go figure," Stacy said breaking the momentary silence. "Now I really AM horny!"

"Well...at least my headaches gone," mom announced.

"Yeah, mine too!" Jessica smiled looking a bit more normal again, though she still looked like something the cat had dragged in...and then fucked.

"Give me a minute sis," I assured her. "The day's just getting started here."

**

While everyone else ran off to actually get cleaned up and straightened up a bit, Stacy and I made our way back to the falls. Though the tiki torches remained along the path leading up to it, we were both surprised that no trace remained whatsoever of anything else. As proficiently as they'd set it all up, they had likewise taken it down again.

"Damn...I was sort of hoping the bed would still be there at least," Stacy said as we made the summit looking about, remembering the crazy evening we'd all experienced together the night before. Even looking down over the cliff-face, there was no evidence that anything had really been disturbed. "I still can't believe you literally fucked me...there," she said pointing at what was now only empty air, the platform we'd stood on no longer there of course. The realization that we really had been only a few feet away from the cliff-face as Stacy technically lost her virginity to me.

"Well at least you do have that," I reminded her. "Something that no one else can lay claim to anyway." She smiled at that, hugging me closer to her, though I moved her back just a bit, worried her sudden enthusiasm might accidentally send us careening over the falls.

"How about, we do it right here then?"

"Sounds like a plan," I told her. We soon spread out our towels into a makeshift blanket for her to lay down on. Once she had, I moved in between her legs, but not before sampling that sweet tasting pussy of hers again. I brought her to the brink of orgasm twice, not quite allowing her to succumb to it however, before finally placing the head of my dick at the opening of her still very puffy looking pussy lips. I teased her with my dick, rubbing the hard swollen head up and down her wet glistening slit, tickling her clit, rubbing the two heads together.

"Enough already! You're teasing me to death here!" She cried out, hunching up, trying to impale herself upon me if I didn't do it to her. Quick as a bunny, I speared her split, driving the entire length of my shaft as deeply into her as I possibly could.

"There. How's that?" I asked as I began thrusting smoothly and easily into her.

"Better...much, much better," she sighed contentedly. And just for a moment, I felt like we really were floating on air.

**

By the time we returned from the falls, David and Dad had returned from their golf outing. But not only that, they were currently standing side-by-side in front of mom as she knelt down there in front of them, holding and sucking their dicks together.

"What's this all about?" Stacy questioned though taking a seat nearby so she could watch.

"This is David's reward for beating me today," Dad answered her.

"David's reward? Looks to me like you're getting rewarded too dad," Stacy asked still somewhat confused, though admittedly, I was wondering the same thing myself.

"Win...win," he chuckled. "I guess in a way, I am. Though this is what he actually wanted to see his mother doing...to both of us. When I told her about the bet, she was more than happy to accommodate his wishes."

"Yeah, we can sort of see that," I spoke, still wondering however. "But...since it is a bet, what did you lose in return for David's winning...besides this." I knew the two of them better than that, and figured that there had to be more to this that what was meeting the eye here.

Dad sheepishly smiled. "Well, I did promise mom that she'd get to fulfill another one of her fantasies later if she paid up on this bet for me. And just so you know, as part of that, we've invited Bob, John, Barbra and Jill over to our island this evening, for a little fun and entertainment. Chris and Jessica have already gone off to get prepared for it, which is why they're not here now," he finished saying. He then looked at his watch. "Should be here in about an hour from now."

"So another party then..." Stacy sighed, though giggling immediately after. "I guess I should just plan on catching up on my sleep tomorrow," she added standing up and preparing to head off to join her sisters.

"Ditto that," I laughed, realizing we most likely had another long erotic, naughty night ahead of us. And though wanting to head off and get cleaned up a bit myself before everyone got here, the sight of mom sucking dad and David's cock together was too good to simply walk away from either. Admittedly, it looked damn fucking hot, especially the way she was doing it, obviously enjoying herself, though certainly pleasuring the two of them as she did it. I was honestly amazed that she could just manage to fit both of their respective cock-heads into her mouth at once, sucking them together, though usually not for too long, needing to both breathe as well as swallow. And I was using this as a way to re-prime my own pump for later this evening when the others finally arrived here. Though that begged another question as well. So far we had kept things pretty much in the family here with a few minor side-trips perhaps. Would things indeed soon go outside of that? It was an interesting thought, and one I was anxious now to discover.

But...I was even more anxious to watch as mom soon drew both dad and David to the brink of orgasm.

"Almost there son," Dad announced, grimacing just a little. "How about you?"

"Oh yeah...yeah," he agreed just about...almost...oh yeah, almost there too," he said looking down at mom, just as she removed both of their dicks, holding them and stroking them together against one another. Amazingly, they both started to cum at almost the same exact instant. Seeing the twin, voluminous spurts as mom directed their spraying cocks against herself, she was soon covered in rivers of white sticky cum, much of which was in her hair as well as in her face, not to mention a great deal of it between her breasts too.

She turned, facing me. An erotic, decadent, obscene sticky mess.

"Well? Care to add your own?" She asked. "Hurry up if you are...I need to start getting ready too."

I was damn fucking tempted. Trust me.

"Maybe a bit later," I found myself saying instead. "After the load I gave Stacy a short while ago, I don't think I'd have all that much to give you myself at the moment."

"Later, I'll have makeup on," mom said smiling through the goo. "But maybe we can plan on doing something else," she smiled trying to wink at me, though the cum more or less kept her from being able to do that.

I simply laughed, turned...and headed back to my own bungalow to get ready for the night ahead.

THE END

www.ingramcontent.com/pod-product-compliance
Lightning Source LLC
LaVergne TN
LVHW011254200326
834410LV00006B/253